LETTERS FROM THE HEART

A Family's Journey of Healing and Hope

ALLAN Q. AMIT

Letters From The Heart
A Family's Journey of Healing and Hope
Copyright © 2024 by Allan Q. Amit. All rights reserved.

ISBN
Paperback: 978-1-966109-06-8
Hardcover: 978-1-966109-07-5
eBook: 978-1-966109-08-2

No part of this publication may be reproduced, stored in a retrieval system or transmitted in any way by any means, electronic, mechanical, photocopy, recording or otherwise without the prior permission of the author except as provided by USA copyright law.

This is a work of fiction. Names, characters, businesses, places, events and incidents are either the products of the author's imagination or used in a fictitious manner. Any resemblance to actual persons, living or dead, or actual events is purely coincidental.

Published in the United States of America.

CONTENTS

Chapter 1	Prologue: The End of an Era	1
Chapter 2	Part I: Uprooted	13
Chapter 3	Part II: Cultural Shockwaves	32
Chapter 4	Part III: Echoes of the Past	45
Chapter 5	Part IV: Building Bridges	61
Chapter 6	Part V: Growing Pains	76
Chapter 7	Part VI: Healing Hearts	89
Chapter 8	Part VII: New Horizons	103
Chapter 9	Epilogue: Letters of Hope	114

CHAPTER 1

PROLOGUE: THE END OF AN ERA

....

The Final Family Dinner

The dining room felt unusually quiet, almost too quiet, as Asher, Ethan, and Allison sat down for what would be their last meal together in their old home. The air was heavy with unspoken emotions—each of them felt it, though none dared to speak. The weight of their shared past lingered, mixing with the uncertainty of the future, and Asher couldn't help but notice how his children's eyes kept darting around the room. They were taking in every familiar detail, trying to capture it in their minds, as if this was the last time they'd ever see it.

Allison, her small frame hunched over her plate, kept glancing at the wall by the kitchen door where their heights had been marked over the years. The last time Asher had measured her was just before they had started packing. Ethan, usually bursting with energy, was unusually quiet. He pushed his food around absentmindedly, lost in his own thoughts, his brow furrowed with emotions he hadn't yet learned to name.

Asher's heart ached, not just for the house they were leaving behind, but for the burden his children carried, for the storm of emotions he knew they were hiding behind their silence. The divorce, the move—they had been through so much. This meal, in so many ways, felt like an ending. But more than that, Asher wanted it to feel like a beginning, even if his children couldn't see it yet. He was determined to help them navigate this new chapter of their lives with as much love and strength as he could muster, even when he wasn't sure if he had enough left for himself.

They ate in near silence, the only sounds coming from the clinking of forks against plates, the soft murmur of their movements, and the occasional sniffle from Allison, who was trying her best not to cry. Asher watched her wipe her nose with the back of her hand, and he felt a pang in his chest. She was only seven—too young to have to deal with something this big. Ethan, at least, had the benefit of being older, but he was struggling in his own way, the pressure of being the older brother, of trying to stay strong, written all over his face.

For a moment, the heaviness lifted as a soft chuckle broke the silence. Allison, in an effort to lighten the mood, had reminded them of a time when the three of them had tried (and failed) to bake a cake for Asher's birthday. Ethan, who had been sulking for most of the meal, allowed a faint smile to creep onto his face, and for a second, things felt normal again. They laughed, remembering the chaos of flour-covered counters and a lopsided cake that had collapsed in the middle.

It was fleeting, but that moment of laughter reminded Asher of something important: their family was still strong, even in the face of change. The home might be different, but the bond between them was unbreakable. Yet, as the meal drew to a close, the reality of what was ahead settled back into the room like an unwelcome guest. Asher knew this was the time. He had been thinking about it for weeks, wondering how to help his children express the things they couldn't say out loud.

He cleared his throat, feeling the weight of the conversation he was about to have. The idea had come to him in a quiet moment of reflection, as he thought about how difficult it had been to talk about their emotions over the past few months. It had always been easier to avoid the hard conversations, to keep things moving so they didn't have to stop and feel the full force of everything they were going through. But they needed to talk, needed a way to let it out, without the pressure of immediate responses or confrontations. And that's when the thought hit him: letters.

"Hey," Asher started, his voice soft but steady. Both Ethan and Allison looked up, sensing the seriousness in their father's tone. "I've been thinking... I know this move has been hard. I know we don't always say what's really on our minds, and that's okay. It's not easy to talk about everything we're feeling."

He paused, glancing at his children to see if they were following him. Ethan's brow furrowed, his curiosity piqued, while Allison's big, tear-stained eyes locked onto his.

"So, I have an idea," Asher continued. "What if we write letters to each other? You don't have to say anything right away, and you can write whenever you feel ready. It doesn't have to be long, just... write whatever you're feeling. It could be about anything. Something that's been on your mind, something you've been worried about, or even just what makes you happy. There's no pressure to talk out loud if you're not ready. We'll just share what's in our hearts when the time feels right."

Ethan shifted in his seat, his initial skepticism giving way to something more thoughtful. Asher could see the wheels turning in his son's mind. Allison, on the other hand, didn't say a word. She looked down at her plate, quietly processing what her father had said.

"I think it could help," Asher added gently. "Sometimes it's easier to write things down than to say them out loud. And that way, we can still talk, even when we don't feel like talking."

For a moment, the table was quiet again. Ethan stared at the candle flickering in the center of the table, his mind clearly miles away, while Allison picked at the last bit of food on her plate, lost in thought. Asher waited, giving them the space they needed to process the idea.

Ethan was the first to break the silence. "So… we just write? And you'll read it when we're ready?"

Asher nodded. "Exactly. You can take your time. You don't have to hand it to me right away. And I'll write too. It's not just for you and Allison—I'll be part of it. We'll all share when we're ready."

Ethan seemed to consider this for a moment, then nodded slowly. Allison still hadn't said much, but Asher could see her wheels turning, the idea beginning to take root in her young mind.

"I like that, Papa," Allison finally whispered, her voice barely audible but filled with the kind of sincerity that only children possess. "I like the letters."

Asher smiled, relief washing over him. He hadn't been sure how they'd respond, but hearing Allison's quiet acceptance made him feel like he was on the right track. This was something they could all do, something that would give them a chance to process their emotions at their own pace. The unspoken pressure to be strong, to act like everything was fine, had been suffocating. Maybe this was the release they needed.

"I'll start tonight," Ethan said, surprising Asher. There was a determination in his son's voice that hadn't been there before. "I think there are some things I need to get out."

Asher nodded, his heart swelling with pride. "Whenever you're ready," he said softly. "I'll be here."

As they cleared the table and began tidying up, the mood felt lighter, as if a small weight had been lifted off their shoulders. The idea of writing letters had opened a door to something new, something healing. For the first time in months, Asher felt a glimmer of hope—not just for himself, but for his children. He knew this journey wasn't over. There would still be difficult days, still moments of doubt and sadness, but they had taken the first step toward something important: healing.

Later that night, as Asher tucked Allison into bed, she looked up at him with wide, innocent eyes. "Papa, will you write me a letter too?" she asked, her voice soft but filled with anticipation.

"Of course I will, sweetheart," Asher whispered, kissing her forehead gently. "I'll write to you, and Ethan, and we'll keep writing to each other for as long as we need."

Allison smiled, a small but genuine smile, and closed her eyes as she nestled into her pillow. Asher stood there for a moment, watching his daughter, feeling the love swell in his chest. This was the beginning of something good. Something healing.

As he left her room, he found Ethan already sitting at his desk, pen in hand, staring at a blank page. Asher didn't say anything, but as he passed by, he placed a gentle hand on his son's shoulder, a silent gesture of support. Ethan looked up, met his father's gaze, and nodded.

And in that small, quiet moment, Asher knew that they would be okay. They had found a way to keep talking, to keep expressing what they couldn't always say out loud. The letters would be their lifeline, their bridge across the uncertainty that still lay ahead.

It was the start of a new chapter—not just in their lives, but in their hearts.

And this time, they would write it together.

PACKING MEMORIES

Asher paused for a moment, his hands resting on the sealed box, feeling the silence settle between the bursts of his children's excitement. The echo of their footsteps in the nearly empty house reminded him that this was real—this chapter was closing, and another was about to begin. The house, once filled with the noise of laughter, arguments, and everyday routine, now felt hollow. Each room whispered memories—of bedtime stories, family dinners, and the once-familiar presence of his ex-wife. He could almost hear her voice in the air, instructing Ethan to clean his room or asking Allison to come to the table. These echoes, though fading, would always linger.

Ethan entered the room, holding a soccer ball, his brows furrowed. "Papa, do you think I can still join a soccer team there?" His voice wavered slightly, a hint of uncertainty breaking through his usual confidence. Asher smiled, a bittersweet tug at his heart. Ethan had always been the one to hold things together, trying to be strong for both his sister and him, but Asher knew the weight of the changes was heavy on his son's young shoulders.

"I'm sure you will, buddy," Asher replied, crouching down to meet Ethan's eyes. "And if not, we'll find a way to keep playing. You'll make new friends, and I promise, things will get better." He ruffled Ethan's hair, but behind the reassuring words, Asher worried. He had no answers for the unknowns awaiting them in the Philippines. But that didn't stop him from trying to offer his son the comfort of certainty.

Allison skipped into the room, clutching her favorite stuffed bunny, its fur worn from years of being dragged along on every adventure. "Papa, are we flying on a really big plane?" she asked, her eyes wide with excitement. She was too young to fully grasp the gravity of their move, but Asher envied her ability to find joy in the smallest things.

"Yes, sweetheart, the biggest plane you've ever seen," Asher replied, scooping her up into his arms, her giggles briefly cutting through the tension. He held her tight for a moment, feeling her small arms wrap around his neck. She was his light, a beacon of innocence in the storm of emotions swirling inside him.

As the sun began to set outside, casting a warm glow through the windows, Asher moved to the doorway and took one last look at the living room. This place had been their home, a shelter during some of their darkest days, but also a place of joy, growth, and love. But it was time to let it go.

"Alright, kids," Asher called, mustering energy he didn't feel. "brush your teeth and head to bed. We've got an early start tomorrow." Ethan and Allison rushed past him, racing to the bathroom, their laughter ringing in his ears as he closed the door behind him, leaving the room in shadows.

In the stillness of the night, long after the kids had fallen asleep, Asher lay awake. His mind raced with thoughts of what lay ahead. The uncertainty gnawed at him—how would they adapt? How would he provide for them in a foreign land? And yet, under the weight of these fears, there was a flicker of hope. They were moving forward, together. And that had to be enough.

He rolled over, glanced at the half-packed suitcase in the corner of the room, and let out a sigh. He didn't know what the future held for them, but as long as he had Ethan and Allison by his side, he knew he'd find a way. Their journey was just beginning.

SAYING GOODBYE TO HOME

As Asher stood in the doorway of the house that had once been their sanctuary, a flood of emotions gripped him, forcing him to pause. His fingers brushed the edge of the doorframe, feeling the cool, familiar surface under his touch. It was strange how a house could feel so alive, even as it stood empty, stripped of its furniture, its pictures, and the laughter that had once filled it. The bare walls seemed to hold their breath, waiting for the inevitable farewell. Asher's breath caught in his throat as the weight of this moment settled in his chest.

With a heavy sigh, he pulled out a notebook, flipping to a fresh page. The blank sheet stared back at him, challenging him to find the right words. For the last few days, Asher had been wrestling with the idea of writing a letter—not to anyone in particular, but to the house itself. This had been their home for years, a place where memories were built, where his children took their first steps, and where he had once believed they would spend the rest of their lives. But life had its own way of redirecting paths, and now, they were about to embark on a journey far from everything they had known.

He wrote with slow, deliberate strokes, penning a letter filled with emotion. "Dear house," he began, his heart pouring into each word. He thanked it for the shelter it had provided, the laughter it had witnessed, and the love it had harbored. But he also spoke of the pain—how it had become a place of silent tension after the divorce, how its rooms felt too large when his ex-wife had left, and how every corner now seemed to echo with the memories they were leaving behind. He expressed hope for the new family that would soon occupy the space, that they might find in it the same comfort and warmth it had once offered them.

> Papa,
>
> This is the last night here in our house, our last goodbye. And I am really scared and sad. I am scared that I might forgot the memories we had here like the pillow fort, running around the house with wife and peeing on the wall fence with him and the noises of barking dogs outside. And I am sad because why do we have to leave. And I don't understand why do we have to. Why does mama have to leave? Does she not love us anymore? And I feel like it is so easy for you to leave this all behind the house, memories, friends and family. I thought we were happy? We were fine but this is not fine at all pa. Why do you keep telling us that everything will be fine when its not. Are you lying? Why can't you and mama say sorry to each other? be together

When he finished, he folded the letter neatly and, with a final glance around the room, tucked it into a small crevice beneath the kitchen sink, a secret message for whoever might one day find it.

His hand lingered on the spot for a moment longer before he rose, exhaling deeply.

Ethan and Allison were quiet, but their presence filled the house in different ways. Ethan, the responsible teenager, had thrown himself into organizing their move. His checklist became his armor, a way to focus on the tangible rather than the emotional. Asher had caught glimpses of him around the house, silently cataloging items, determining what to keep and what to discard. It was as if he believed that if he could just organize everything perfectly, the chaos of their lives might also fall into place.

Ethan's eyes, however, betrayed him. When Asher saw his son from across the room, meticulously wrapping a set of books, his hands moved with mechanical precision, but his eyes were distant, glossed with thoughts he refused to share. He was holding it together, as he always did. Ever since the divorce, Ethan had felt the pressure of being the man of the house, stepping into shoes far too big for him to fill. Asher knew the weight his son carried and wished he could take it from him, but no words had been able to bridge the gap that had slowly grown between them.

Allison, on the other hand, made no effort to hide her feelings. She stood in the kitchen, her small hand tracing the faded pencil marks on the doorframe where her height had been recorded over the years. Each mark represented a snapshot of time—her growth measured in inches, her childhood immortalized in these fleeting strokes. Tears rolled silently down her cheeks as she glanced up at Asher, her lip trembling.

"Papa," she whispered, her voice barely audible over the silence of the empty house, "I don't want to leave this behind."

Asher knelt beside her, pulling her into his arms. "I know, sweetheart," he said softly, feeling the tightness in his chest intensify. "I don't want to leave it behind either. But we'll take the memories with us. We'll always have those."

"But what about Mama?" she asked, her voice breaking. "What if we forget her?"

Asher's heart clenched. He didn't have a simple answer for that. How could he assure her that memories of her mother would stay alive, even as they moved to a new place, a new life? He gently wiped her tears and kissed the top of her head. "We won't forget her," he promised. "She'll always be a part of us, no matter where we are. And wherever we go, we'll make new memories together, just like we did here."

They stayed like that for a few moments, father and daughter, bound by the grief of their shared loss and the uncertainty of the future. Asher felt a surge of love for his children, a fierce protective instinct rising within him. He didn't know what lay ahead, but he knew that as long as they had each other, they would figure it out.

Later, as the day drew to a close and the sun began to set, casting long shadows across the floor, the three of them gathered in the living room—just as they had countless times before. Only this time, there were no comfortable couches to sink into, no familiar warmth from the fireplace. They sat on the hardwood floor, the last boxes packed and waiting by the door. This was it. The final goodbye.

Asher cleared his throat, unsure how to start. "I thought..." he hesitated, searching for the right words. "I thought we could all share our favorite memories of this place before we go."

Ethan, always the one to resist emotional displays, rolled his eyes slightly but said nothing. Allison, ever the emotional heart of the family, nodded eagerly, though her face still showed traces of sadness.

"I'll go first," Asher said, glancing around the room. "I think my favorite memory is the time we built that ridiculous fort with all the couch cushions and blankets. Do you remember? We turned the entire living room into a fortress, and we ended up spending the whole weekend in there, pretending we were on some grand adventure." He smiled, the memory warming his heart. "We even tried to sleep in it, but the whole thing collapsed in the middle of the night."

Ethan snorted, a small smile tugging at his lips. "Yeah, that was fun," he admitted. "I remember that."

"Me too!" Allison chimed in, her eyes brightening for the first time in hours. "I thought we were really going to live in that fort forever!"

Asher laughed, ruffling her hair. "That's the magic of it, kiddo. We can take that adventure with us, wherever we go."

There was a pause, then Ethan spoke up, surprising both Asher and Allison. "My favorite memory," he said, his voice quieter, more thoughtful, "was when we all went camping in the backyard. Mama made us those s'mores, and we stayed up late watching the stars." His gaze dropped to the floor, his voice faltering slightly. "It felt like we were the only ones in the world, you know? Just the four of us. Everything felt...right."

Asher felt a lump rise in his throat but managed to keep his voice steady. "That was a special night," he agreed softly. "One of the best."

Allison sniffled, her small hand reaching for Ethan's. "My favorite memory was when we had that rainy day and stayed home from school. We played inside, made pillow forts, and watched movies all day. Then we had hot chocolate, and we all cuddled up together on the couch." Her voice wavered. "It was perfect."

Asher swallowed hard, his chest tightening as the weight of their memories settled around them. This house had seen so much joy, so much love, and even the pain they had endured within its walls couldn't tarnish those moments. It had been their home, a witness to their lives.

But now, it was time to let go.

They sat in silence for a while longer, each lost in their thoughts, until finally, Asher stood. "Come on," he said, his voice gentle but firm. "It's time."

Ethan and Allison stood, their faces a mixture of sadness and determination. Together, they walked to the front door, their footsteps slow and deliberate. Asher hesitated for a moment, then turned the key in the lock for the last time. The click of the door echoed through the empty house, and with a final glance, they stepped outside.

The air was cool, and the sky had turned a deep orange as the sun dipped below the horizon. Asher felt a strange sense of peace settle over him. They had said their goodbyes, shared their memories, and now it was time to look ahead.

As they walked toward the car, Asher took one last look at the house. It would always be a part of them, a chapter in their story. But the next chapter was waiting to be written.

Ethan climbed into the backseat, his headphones already in place, while Allison snuggled into her favorite blanket beside him. Asher took his seat in the driver's seat, the keys jingling in his hand. He glanced in the rearview mirror, catching a glimpse of his children in the back.

They were leaving behind so much, but they had each other.

He started the engine, the car rumbling to life, and as they pulled away from the house, Asher felt a flicker of hope stir in his chest. The road ahead was uncertain, filled with unknowns, but for the first time in a long while, he felt like they were ready for it.

Together, they would face whatever came next.

CHAPTER 2
PART I: UPROOTED

....

Asher's First Letter: A New Beginning

Dear Ethan and Allison,

As I sit here in the quiet of our small apartment, watching the last rays of sunlight stretch across the skyline of this bustling city, I feel the weight of everything that has brought us to this moment. It's been two weeks since we landed in the Philippines, and already it feels like a lifetime of change has washed over us. The hum of the streets below, the cacophony of unfamiliar voices, the scent of food I still don't know the name of—it's all a constant reminder that we are far from the life we once knew.

But, as disorienting as it is, there's something about this place that feels... like a promise. A promise of something different, something new. I see it in the way the sunlight glints off the glass of our apartment window. I hear it in the faint music that drifts up from the streets. It's like the universe is whispering to us, reminding us that despite the fear, despite the uncertainty, there is hope.

Ethan, Allison, I know this journey hasn't been easy for either of you. How could it be? We uprooted everything—your friends, your school, the comfort of the familiar. I see it in your eyes, the quiet sadness, the unspoken grief. We lost something back in Los Angeles, something deep, and no new city, no matter how vibrant, can take away the pain of that. Your mother's absence lingers with us, like a shadow, always present even when we don't talk about it.

Ethan, you're trying to be brave. I see it in the way you mask your emotions with quiet determination, how you dive into your schoolwork as if solving equations or memorizing facts could somehow make the hurt go away. I see it in how you hold Allison's hand when you think I'm not looking, trying to reassure her, trying to be strong for her. You're more like me than you know, always trying to shoulder the world's weight without ever asking for help. But you don't have to be the protector all the time. It's okay to feel scared, to feel lost. It's okay to cry. I'm here for you, and I'll always be.

And Allison, my sweet, curious Allison. I watch you as you explore this new world with wide eyes, every corner of this city a new adventure for you. You ask me a hundred questions about everything, and I try my best to answer, even though sometimes I'm just as unsure as you are. But behind your curiosity, I see the moments when your smile fades, when you look up at me and ask about Mama, when you wonder why she's not here with us, why everything had to change. Those are the moments that break my heart, because no answer I give you will ever feel enough. But know this—your mother's love is still with us, always. It lives in the stories we tell, in the memories we share, in the way we carry her with us every single day.

I wanted to write this letter to you both because words have always been my way of making sense of the world. When I write, I feel like I can unravel the chaos of life and find meaning in it, and right now, life feels like a puzzle I'm still trying to figure out. But what I do know is this: This move, this upheaval, isn't just about leaving behind what we lost. It's about finding out who we are, and who we can become. We didn't just come to the Philippines to escape our past—we came here to build a new future.

Every day, as I watch you both navigate this new place, I see sparks of resilience in you. Ethan, I see the way you observe everything, taking mental notes, figuring out how to fit in while still holding on to who you are. And Allison, your endless energy, your unstoppable curiosity—it reminds me that this isn't just a hard time, it's a time of growth. We are in a new country, yes, but this is also a chance for us to rediscover joy. It's a chance to heal.

This city, with all its noise and chaos, is our blank slate. It's where we'll rewrite the story of us—of our family. I know it's not going to be easy. We'll face challenges. There will be days when it feels like everything is too much, when the homesickness will feel unbearable, when the memories of our old life will claw at us, threatening to pull us under. But I also know that we have something stronger than any of those challenges. We have each other.

And that, Ethan and Allison, is the heart of everything. We have each other. That bond—the bond of family—is our greatest strength. It's what will carry us through the hardest days and lift us in the best of times. We're not alone in this journey. We'll find our way, together.

As I sit here writing this, I think back to all the little moments we've already shared in this new place. The other day, Ethan, when you figured out how to bargain at the market, your face lighting up with pride when you got us a better deal than I ever could have? Or, Allison, when you found that stray cat near the apartment, and you spent hours trying to coax it into letting you pet it? You both amaze me every day with your ability to adapt, to find light in the dark. You inspire me to keep going, even when I'm unsure of the path ahead.

The coming days will test us, there's no doubt about that. You'll start new schools soon, meet new friends, and face the challenge of learning in an environment that's still foreign to you. There will be times when you'll feel out of place, like you don't belong, but I want you to remember something important—home isn't a place. It's not a city or a house or even a country. Home is where we are, together. Home is the love we share, the memories we create, the laughter that bubbles up even on the hardest days. And as long as we're together, we will always be home.

This letter is a reminder to all of us that this is just the beginning of a new chapter. We are not defined by the past we've left behind, nor by the mistakes or the pain that came before. We are defined by how we move forward, by the love we carry, and by the strength we show in the face of uncertainty. Every day is a step toward healing. Every new experience is a chance to grow.

So, Ethan and Allison, let's embrace this adventure with open hearts. Let's make new friends, explore new places, and create new memories. Let's keep your mother's spirit alive in the way we live, in the way we love, in the way we laugh. She is with us, always.

I promise you both that I will be here every step of the way. I may not have all the answers—I'm still learning too—but I will never stop trying. I will never stop showing up for you, fighting for you, loving you. This life we are building, it's ours. And it's going to be beautiful.

With all my love,
Papa

As Asher folded the letter, he felt the weight of his own words sink into him. The fears, the doubts, the hopes—it was all there, laid bare in ink on the page. He hadn't planned to write something so emotional, but once he started, the floodgates opened. He couldn't stop himself from telling Ethan and Allison everything he felt, everything that had been bottled up since the move.

He slid the letter into an envelope and tucked it away in a drawer. Maybe he wouldn't give it to them right away. Maybe it would be something for the future, when they needed to be reminded of this moment, when they were older and could look back on this time with new eyes. But for now, the act of writing it had been enough. It had been his way of grounding himself, of acknowledging that this journey wasn't just for them—it was for him too.

    Standing from the table, Asher walked to the window. The city buzzed with life below, a stark contrast to the quiet of their old home in Los Angeles. He didn't know what the future held, but for the first time in a long time, he felt like that was okay. He didn't need to know. All that mattered was that they were together, and that they had the strength to keep moving forward, one day at a time.

> 1999_
>
> Everything feels strange here from language to people everything feels weird. It feels like I'm in a movie where I go somewhere far away to start a new peaceful life away from everything... a reset. but this is not my reality. I didn't chose to be here and I also don't have a choice funny because I feel like a stranger a foreigner— and it doesn't feel right. It's really hard adapting to this new world. And doesn't make sense how I could und...

    The sun had set, but the horizon still glowed with the promise of tomorrow. Asher smiled to himself, a small, hopeful smile. Their story was far from over—it was only just beginning.

ETHAN'S JOURNAL: STRANGER IN A STRANGE LAND

Dear Journal,

I never thought I'd find myself here, sitting in this cramped apartment, trying to make sense of a life that feels like it belongs to someone else. It's been three months since Papa, Allison, and I moved to the Philippines, and every single day feels like I'm wading through some strange, sticky fog. Nothing here feels like home. The sights, the smells, the sounds—they're all so... *different*. Even the air here feels thick, like it's got something heavy in it, making it hard to breathe sometimes. I didn't think it would hit me this hard. I didn't think I'd feel like such a stranger in my own life.

    I miss California. I miss the way the sky turned orange at sunset, how the streets in our old neighborhood felt alive but familiar, not overwhelming like the streets here. There's always noise, like the city never sleeps. People shouting, jeepneys honking, vendors selling food I don't even recognize. And the smells—sometimes they're amazing, like fried chicken and garlic rice, but then other times... it's too much. It's all too much. I miss the quiet of home, where everything was predictable. Where I could walk down the street and wave at neighbors who knew my name, who didn't look at me like I was some kind of curiosity.

    School is... well, it's a battlefield. Not in the way you'd think, though. No one's bullying me, exactly. It's more like I'm invisible. No one really knows what to make of me. I can see it in their eyes when I walk down the hallway—the other kids glance at me, curious but cautious, like I'm some exotic animal that wandered in from the wrong exhibit. They talk about things I don't understand, references to TV shows and jokes that go way over my head. It's like I'm living in a bubble, watching everything happen on the outside but unable to break through.

And the language—God, the language. Tagalog spills out of their mouths like water, fast and flowing, and I'm stuck trying to catch a word here or there, like fishing for raindrops in a storm. Sometimes I feel like I'm drowning in it. I sit in class and try to keep up, nodding like I understand, but most of the time, I don't. I hear kids laughing, probably making fun of me when I stumble over a simple phrase. I want to tell them that I'm not an idiot, that I used to be one of the smartest kids in my class back home. But now... now I feel stupid.

There are moments, though. Little flashes of light in the darkness. Like this one time, during lunch, when a girl named Paula sat with me. I was sitting by myself, pretending not to notice how everyone else was grouped in tight circles, talking and laughing. And then, out of nowhere, Paula plopped down next to me with her tray and just... started talking. In English. Not perfect English, but good enough. She asked me about California, about what it's like to live in America. I could tell she was nervous, but in that moment, I felt something I hadn't felt in a long time—a connection. I told her about In-N-Out burgers, about the beaches, about how much I missed the smell of ocean air. For the first time since we got here, I wasn't just that weird new kid. I was someone with a story worth sharing.

But those moments are rare. Most of the time, I feel like I'm drifting, just trying to hold on to something solid. Papa... he's trying so hard, I can see it. The way he carries this weight on his shoulders, like he's responsible for everything. I catch him sometimes, staring out the window like he's lost, like he's not sure he made the right decision bringing us here. But he doesn't say it. He never says it. He tries to keep everything together for Allison and me, but I see the worry lines etched deeper into his face every day. And it scares me. Because if Papa's not sure, then what does that mean for us?

Allison... she's having the hardest time, I think. She puts on a brave face during the day, asking a million questions like she always does, exploring the newness of everything like it's an adventure.

But at night, when she thinks no one can hear, I can hear her crying in her room. She misses Mama. I do too, but I don't know how to fill that space for her. How am I supposed to be strong when I don't even feel strong myself? I want to tell her that everything will be okay, that this will get easier, but I don't know if I believe it. We're all just trying to stay afloat in this new world that doesn't feel like ours yet.

It's weird, because sometimes I wonder if this feeling of being out of place will ever go away. Will this ever feel like home? Or will I always feel like a visitor in someone else's life? There are these moments, though, where I catch a glimpse of something—something that feels like it *could* be home, eventually. Like when we all had dinner at that little street stall last weekend. The food was so different from what we used to have, but somehow, sitting there with Papa and Allison, laughing at how spicy the food was, it felt... normal. It felt like we were a family again, not just three people trying to survive.

And then there's the language. It's hard, but there are times when I get it. Like the other day, I was listening to some kids talking in Tagalog, and for once, I didn't feel completely lost. I understood just enough to know they weren't talking about me. They were just talking. I even caught myself laughing at one of their jokes—something about a teacher and a chalkboard. It wasn't much, but it felt like progress. Like maybe this invisible wall between me and everyone else is starting to crack, just a little.

But then, just when I think I'm making progress, something happens to remind me how far I still have to go. Like today, when the teacher called on me to answer a question in Tagalog. I froze. Everyone's eyes were on me, waiting. I tried to say something, anything, but the words got tangled up in my mouth, and all I managed was this awkward stammer before the teacher moved on, trying to save me from further embarrassment. The kids snickered, and I felt that familiar flush of heat rise to my cheeks. It's moments like that that make me wonder if I'll ever really fit in here. If I'll ever stop feeling like the outsider.

Still, I have to believe that this is temporary. I have to believe that one day, it'll get easier. I tell myself that every morning when I wake up and face another day of school, another day of trying to fit into this life that feels like it belongs to someone else. I tell myself that I'm doing this for Papa and Allison, that I have to be strong for them. I see how much Papa is giving up for us, how much he's trying to make this work. He doesn't say it, but I know he's scared too. I can't let him down. And Allison… she looks up to me. She needs me to be strong, even when I don't feel strong. Especially when I don't feel strong.

So, I keep going. One day at a time. One awkward, uncomfortable, exhausting day at a time. And maybe, just maybe, things will start to feel right. Maybe one day I'll wake up and this place will feel like home, instead of some foreign land where I'm just passing through. Maybe the kids at school will stop seeing me as the weird American and start seeing me as just… me. Maybe Papa will stop looking so worried all the time, and Allison will stop crying at night. Maybe one day, we'll all feel like we belong here.

But until then, I'll keep writing. I'll keep trying. I'll keep holding on to those little moments—the kind classmate, the laugh I understand, the taste of something familiar in the middle of all this strangeness. Those moments are what keep me going, what give me hope. And for now, hope is enough.

Yours,
Ethan

Ethan closed the journal and stared at the cover for a long time. The words he had just written echoed in his mind, and for the first time in a while, he felt a strange sense of calm. It wasn't much, but it was something—a way to make sense of the mess swirling inside him. Writing it all down had made it feel a little less overwhelming, like he could see the pieces of his life more clearly.

He stood up and walked to the window, looking out at the city below. The sun was setting, casting a warm, golden glow over the streets. He watched as people bustled about, their voices mingling with the distant hum of traffic. It was all so different from home, and yet… there was something about it that felt alive, full of possibility.

Ethan didn't know what tomorrow would bring, but for the first time in a long time, he didn't feel as scared. He had his family. He had his journal. And maybe, just maybe, he had the beginnings of something new—a life he could start to call his own.

With a small, hopeful smile, Ethan turned away from the window and went to find Papa and Allison. It was time to start living, one day at a time.

ALLISON'S LETTER: MISSING MAMA AND HOME

Papa,

I don't really know how to say this, so I guess I'll just write it down like you always tell me to do when my feelings are too big. I miss Mama. I miss her so much that sometimes it feels like my heart can't hold all the missing anymore. And I miss our old house, too. Everything here is just so… different. The air smells different, the food tastes different, and I don't like how loud it always is outside. I miss the quiet of our home, and I miss the way Mama's laugh filled up the whole house, like it was warm sunshine on a cold day.

Sometimes, I wake up in the middle of the night, and for a second, I forget where I am. My eyes are still all sleepy, and I think I'm back in my old room. You know, the one with the yellow walls and the posters on the ceiling? For just a tiny moment, I feel safe again, like everything's how it used to be, and then I remember. I remember that we're not there anymore. And then it feels like someone took away my safe place, like a part of me is still back in that room, waiting for everything to go back to normal.

I know you're trying your best, Papa, and I love you for it. I see how hard you're working to make this place feel like home. But it's not the same. It's not even close. I miss the way Mama used to brush my hair before school, and how she'd always smile at me in the morning, even when I didn't feel like smiling back. It's silly, I know, but I miss the way she always made breakfast just right—pancakes that weren't too crispy or too soft. Mama always seemed to know exactly what I needed, even when I didn't.

The other day, when we were at the supermarket, I saw a woman who looked just like her from behind. She had the same curly hair and was wearing a green sweater, like the one Mama used to wear. My heart did this weird thing—it skipped a beat, and I thought for just one crazy second, "It's her!" I almost ran up to her, but then I realized it wasn't. It wasn't her, and it never will be her, and that's when everything came crashing down again. It's like losing her over and over, Papa. Every day, it feels like I'm losing her all over again.

Papa,

I don't know what to say but sometimes I feel like I don't belong here in the Philippines every time I try to say something in tagalog I mess up I miss our old home I miss the backyard I miss mama I miss when she would make my pancakes

I don't really know how to say this without sounding like I'm complaining, but I'm trying to be strong. I really am. I know that's what you want, and I want it too. I don't want to make things harder for you, but sometimes it's just too much. The new school is scary. The kids are nice, I guess, but I don't understand what they're saying half the time, and I feel like they look at me funny. I try to talk to them, but my words come out all wrong, and I get so embarrassed that I just stop talking. I wish I could be brave like you, but right now, I feel really small. Too small for this big, new world we're in.

And the language... It's hard, Papa. I'm trying, I really am, but my mouth can't seem to get the words right. They feel too big for my tongue, and sometimes, the kids laugh when I try to say something in Tagalog. I know they don't mean to be mean, but it makes me feel like I'll never belong. I miss my friends back home. I miss speaking in a way that doesn't make me feel like I'm messing up all the time.

Even the little things feel too much. I miss the neighbors, even grumpy Mr. Stevens with his scratchy voice. I miss our backyard, where I used to play after school. And I miss the dog next door—you know, the one that always barked at nothing? He used to annoy me so much, but now... I even miss that. How weird is that? I miss everything, even the things I didn't like. Does that make sense?

I know you said this move is for the best. I know you've told me a thousand times that we're starting fresh, that this is our chance to make something new and good. But sometimes, it doesn't feel like that at all. Right now, it just feels like we've left behind everything that made us us. Like who we were, who I was, is still stuck in that old house, waiting for us to come back. How do we start over when so much of who we are is still back there? How can I make this place my home when it feels like I don't belong here?

I don't know the answer. I wish I did. But I'm trying, Papa. I'm trying really hard. I just miss Mama. I miss home. And I miss the way things used to be.

Letters From The Heart

Love,
Allison

Allison sat back after finishing the letter, her small hands gripping the paper tightly. Her eyes stung with unshed tears, but she held them back. She didn't want to cry anymore. Crying hadn't helped, and it wouldn't bring Mama back or make their old life magically reappear. It just left her feeling emptier, more lost.

She looked out the small window of their apartment. The streets below were filled with people, so many people, and yet Allison had never felt more alone. The sky was a deep, cloudy gray, nothing like the clear blue skies back home. There, the sun seemed to shine differently, warmer, friendlier. Here, everything felt muted, unfamiliar.

She folded the letter carefully and placed it in her dresser drawer, tucking it beneath her favorite shirt—the one Mama had bought her before they moved. She thought about giving the letter to Papa, but something stopped her. What if it made him sad? She didn't want that. He was already trying so hard to make everything okay. She didn't want him to worry even more.

Allison slipped off her bed and padded quietly to the living room, where Papa sat at the kitchen table, his laptop open and papers spread around him. He looked tired, his eyes shadowed with worry. Allison didn't want to add to that.

"Papa?" she asked softly, and he looked up from his work, forcing a smile.

"Yes, sweetheart?"

"Can I sit with you?"

He smiled, the weariness in his eyes lifting just a little. "Of course."

She climbed into his lap, resting her head on his chest, and for a moment, the world didn't feel so big. His arms wrapped around her, and she closed her eyes, listening to the steady beat of his heart.

It was the sound that made everything feel right, even when nothing else did.

"I miss her too, you know," Papa whispered, his voice thick. "Every day."

Allison swallowed, her throat tight. She nodded against his chest, not trusting herself to speak.

"We're going to be okay," he said, his voice stronger now, more certain. "It's going to take time, but we'll find our way."

"Do you really think so?" she asked, her voice small.

"I know so," Papa replied, squeezing her gently. "We have each other, and that's what matters most. We'll make a new home here. It won't be the same, but it'll be ours."

Allison stayed there in his arms, letting his words settle over her like a warm blanket. She still missed Mama. She still missed home. But in that moment, wrapped up in Papa's embrace, she started to believe that maybe—just maybe—things could get better.

Later that night, after Papa had kissed her goodnight and tucked her in, Allison lay awake, staring at the ceiling. The soft hum of the city drifted in through the open window, mixing with the sound of her own breathing. She thought about Mama, about the way her laugh used to fill the house with warmth, about the way she used to brush her hair in the mornings, about the way everything felt right when she was near.

But then Allison thought about what Papa had said. About finding a new home here, about making this place theirs. It was hard to imagine right now, but maybe, just maybe, it was possible. Maybe they could build something new, something that didn't erase the past but added to it.

Allison rolled over, pulling the blanket up to her chin. She closed her eyes and pictured Mama's face, the way she smiled, the way her eyes crinkled at the corners when she was happy.

"I won't forget you," Allison whispered into the darkness. "I promise."

And as she drifted off to sleep, for the first time in what felt like forever, she felt a tiny spark of hope flicker inside her. It was small, but it was enough to hold onto.

After writing her letter, Allison found herself feeling a little lighter, as if putting all her thoughts down on paper had eased the weight of missing Mama and their old life. The next day, she woke up early, the morning light spilling through the thin curtains of their new apartment. She rolled over, staring at the ceiling, and something stirred inside her—maybe it was the memory of her letter, or maybe it was something Papa had said the night before. They *could* make this place home. Maybe not the same home as before, but a different one.

That morning, Papa had a surprise for them.

"Get dressed, kids. We're going out today," Papa announced at breakfast, a rare twinkle of excitement in his eyes.

Ethan raised an eyebrow, still groggy from sleep. "Where are we going?"

"You'll see," Papa replied, a smile playing on his lips. "There's a lot of this city we haven't explored yet, and I think it's time we did."

Allison perked up, feeling a flutter of curiosity. The city felt overwhelming most of the time, but there was something about Papa's enthusiasm that made her want to see it through his eyes. Maybe this place had its own kind of magic, waiting to be discovered.

As they stepped out onto the bustling streets of Manila, the air was thick with humidity, but it was also alive with energy. Everywhere Allison looked, there was movement—people crisscrossing the sidewalks, colorful jeepneys weaving through traffic, vendors calling out from their stalls. The sights and sounds were dizzying, but instead of feeling overwhelmed, today she felt a spark of something else. Was it excitement?

Their first stop was the local market, a place so vibrant and full of life that Allison couldn't help but stare in awe. The smell of grilled meat and garlic filled the air, and rows of stalls overflowed with fruits in colors she had never seen before—purple, orange, green, all mixed together like a painting. Vendors shouted playfully at them, beckoning them to try their food, and Papa laughed, saying something in Tagalog that made the vendors smile.

"What's that?" Allison asked, pointing to a fruit that looked like it was covered in spikes.

"That's *rambutan*," Papa explained, picking one up and offering it to her. "It's sweet inside, trust me."

She hesitated for a moment but took it, peeling back the rough skin to reveal the soft, white flesh inside. She bit into it, and her eyes widened. It was sweet, like candy, but fresh and juicy. She grinned at Papa, who smiled back, pleased.

"This place smells amazing," Ethan muttered, clearly torn between his typical teenage skepticism and his growing curiosity. "What's that?" He pointed to a sizzling skewer of meat at a nearby stand.

"That, my boy, is *isaw*—grilled chicken intestines," Papa said with a grin.

Ethan recoiled slightly. "Intestines?"

"Trust me, it's good," Papa laughed, grabbing a skewer and taking a bite, his eyes lighting up as he chewed. "This is the real stuff. Want to try?"

Ethan wrinkled his nose but took a tiny bite, and to his surprise, his expression changed. "It's actually... not bad."

Papa clapped him on the back. "See? Told you. You've got to keep an open mind here. The food might seem strange at first, but it's delicious once you give it a chance."

As they continued through the market, they tried all sorts of new things—*bibingka*, a rice cake that was soft and sweet, and *balut*, a delicacy that made Ethan gag but had Papa laughing so hard he nearly dropped it. Allison stayed close to Papa, her eyes wide as she took in the bright, unfamiliar world around her. Every corner was filled with something new—a dish she'd never seen, a smell she'd never experienced. It was all strange, but not in a bad way. It was strange in a way that made her curious, made her want to see more.

After the market, Papa had another surprise for them.

"We're going somewhere special now," he said, ushering them toward a jeepney, a brightly painted open-air bus that Ethan had been eyeing suspiciously since they'd arrived in Manila.

"Do we have to ride *that*?" Ethan asked, eyeing the jeepney with a mix of horror and fascination.

"Yes, we do," Papa replied cheerfully. "It's the best way to get around. And besides, it's an adventure."

They climbed into the jeepney, squeezing in with locals who eyed them curiously but smiled in a friendly way. Allison giggled as they bumped along the crowded streets, feeling like they were part of the city's rhythm, part of its heartbeat. The wind rushed past her face as the jeepney wound its way through the narrow roads, and for the first time, she didn't feel like a stranger. She felt like she was part of something bigger.

When they finally reached their destination, Allison's eyes widened. Papa had brought them to *Rizal Park*, a huge green space in the middle of the city. It was bustling with families, children running around, and vendors selling cotton candy and balloons.

"This is where you can see the city and feel its history," Papa said, his voice soft but filled with meaning. "This place has been here for hundreds of years. It's where the people come to remember who they are."

Allison and Ethan wandered through the park, their curiosity pulling them in every direction. Allison spotted a group of kids flying colorful kites near a pond, and she couldn't resist joining them. Ethan, for his part, found himself drawn to the giant statue of José Rizal, the national hero of the Philippines, standing tall and proud in the middle of the park.

"Who's that?" Ethan asked, glancing at the statue.

"That's Rizal," Papa said, standing beside him. "He fought for the Philippines' independence. He's a symbol of the strength and bravery of this country."

Ethan stared at the statue, his expression thoughtful. "He looks... strong."

"He was," Papa said quietly. "And so are you."

Ethan looked up at him, surprised by the compliment, but said nothing. Instead, he simply nodded, and the two of them stood there, side by side, gazing at the monument in silence.

As the sun began to set over the park, casting a golden glow across the trees and statues, Allison felt something shift inside her. This place was different—so different from home—but it wasn't all bad. There was something beautiful about it, something alive. The food, the people, the park, the way the city seemed to pulse with energy—it was all starting to feel less scary. She glanced at Ethan, who seemed more relaxed now, his usual guarded expression softening as he watched kids play soccer nearby.

"Papa," Allison said quietly, tugging at his hand.

"Yes, sweetheart?"

"I think I like it here."

Papa's smile was small but filled with emotion. He knelt down beside her and cupped her face in his hands, his eyes shining with a mixture of relief and love. "I'm glad, Allison. I'm really glad."

Ethan didn't say anything, but when Papa turned to him with a questioning look, he shrugged and said, "Yeah... it's okay, I guess."

Papa ruffled his hair, a rare moment of playfulness. "You'll see. It'll feel like home before you know it."

Allison wasn't sure if that was true yet, but for the first time, she didn't feel the gnawing homesickness that had been following her like a shadow. The day had been filled with so many new experiences, and though it wasn't the same as home, it was starting to feel like *something*. Maybe, just maybe, they could build a new life here. A different life, but one that could still be good.

As they made their way back to the jeepney, the sky turning a deep shade of purple, Allison leaned her head on Papa's shoulder, her heart a little lighter. She didn't know what tomorrow would bring, but today had been enough. And for now, that was all she needed.

That night, as Allison lay in bed, her thoughts drifted back to the market, to the sweet taste of rambutan and the way the jeepney had bounced along the streets. She thought about Rizal Park and the kids with their kites, and how, for the first time, she had laughed and played without thinking about what she had left behind. Maybe she wasn't ready to call this place home just yet, but she could feel herself getting closer to it.

As she closed her eyes, she whispered to herself, "Maybe tomorrow, it will feel even better." And with that thought, she drifted off to sleep, dreaming of new adventures in this strange, beautiful place that was slowly becoming a part of her.

CHAPTER 3
PART II: CULTURAL SHOCKWAVES

....

Language Barriers and Misunderstandings

The first few weeks in their new home felt like stepping into a maze where every turn revealed a new challenge. For Asher, Ethan, and Allison, language was more than just a tool for communication—it was the key to survival. Each conversation, each interaction was a puzzle, pieced together with gestures, nods, and the occasional fragment of a phrase. More often than not, they found themselves lost in translation.

The air in Manila buzzed with conversations they couldn't fully grasp. Tagalog flowed like music through the streets—rapid, rhythmic, punctuated by words that slipped through their fingers no matter how hard they tried to catch them. Asher had anticipated some difficulty, but the reality of the language barrier was far more isolating than he had imagined. Adapting to the Philippines had always seemed like it would be an uphill battle, but the daily struggle to understand and be understood felt like walking through a thick fog. He wasn't just a man in a new country; he was a man struggling to find his voice in it.

Work became one of the most frustrating arenas for Asher. It wasn't just the words that tripped him up; it was the cultural nuances behind them. Meetings were often filled with idiomatic expressions, jokes, and references that left him nodding along, trying to appear as though he understood. But inside, he felt a growing frustration. He would jot down notes, circle unfamiliar phrases, and try to piece together the context later, but the sting of not being able to fully participate gnawed at him. Asher wasn't used to being a bystander in his own life, yet here, in this new place, that's exactly how he felt.

One afternoon, after a particularly difficult meeting, Asher stood by the office window, watching the city pulse beneath him. Manila was alive with activity—jeepneys crisscrossed the streets, street vendors called out to passersby, and the hum of conversations filled the air. But it was all happening without him. The feeling of disconnect weighed heavily on his shoulders. He wasn't just navigating a new job; he was trying to navigate a whole new world.

"You look lost," Mateo's voice broke through Asher's thoughts. His colleague's Tagalog accent was thick but his tone warm, understanding. Mateo had been working with Asher since his arrival, always patient, always willing to help him find his footing.

"I feel lost," Asher admitted, running a hand through his hair. "I don't understand half of what's being said in these meetings. It's like everyone's speaking in code."

Mateo chuckled softly. "That's because we are. It's local slang, things you'll pick up eventually. Don't worry, Asher. It's hard at first, but you'll get there. It just takes time."

Time. Asher knew Mateo was right, but time felt like a luxury he couldn't afford. The pressure to prove himself, to find his place both in the workplace and in this new country, weighed on him. Still, Mateo's patience and his willingness to explain cultural nuances gave Asher a glimmer of hope. Not everything was lost in translation. The small gestures of kindness—like Mateo slowing down to explain a confusing phrase—reminded Asher that he wasn't completely alone in this journey.

Yet the language barrier went beyond words and meetings. Asher was learning that even small, seemingly insignificant actions could carry different meanings here. One day, after a work meeting, he found himself walking down the hallway with Mae, a senior manager at the company. Out of habit, Asher reached the door first and held it open for her. Mae hesitated, a slight look of confusion crossing her face, before offering him a tight smile as she passed through.

Later, during a coffee break, Mateo sidled up to Asher with a knowing grin. "You know, holding the door for women here... it can sometimes be seen as more than just politeness. It can be interpreted as romantic interest."

Asher blinked, taken aback. "Wait, what? I was just being polite."

Mateo laughed. "I know, man. But here, certain gestures can have different meanings. It's one of those little cultural things that trips people up. Don't worry—Mae probably didn't think much of it, but it's good to know."

Asher felt his face flush with embarrassment. Something as simple as opening a door, a gesture he hadn't thought twice about, suddenly carried weight he hadn't intended. He felt as though he was constantly misreading the signals around him, always one step behind in understanding the unspoken rules of this new culture.

The next few days, Asher found himself second-guessing his actions, unsure if his attempts at politeness were being misinterpreted. He had always considered himself culturally sensitive, but here, in the Philippines, he was realizing there were layers to communication he had never encountered before. It wasn't just about words; it was about body language, subtle cues, and the rhythm of interactions. Whether it was avoiding prolonged eye contact, speaking with a softer tone, or knowing when to step back, every action felt like part of an intricate dance he was only just learning.

Despite these missteps, Asher's work life wasn't all frustration. Little by little, he began to notice the small victories. He started picking up on the slang Mateo had mentioned, understanding a little more of the conversation in meetings each day. He even found himself laughing along with jokes he wouldn't have understood a week earlier. Progress was slow, but it was happening.

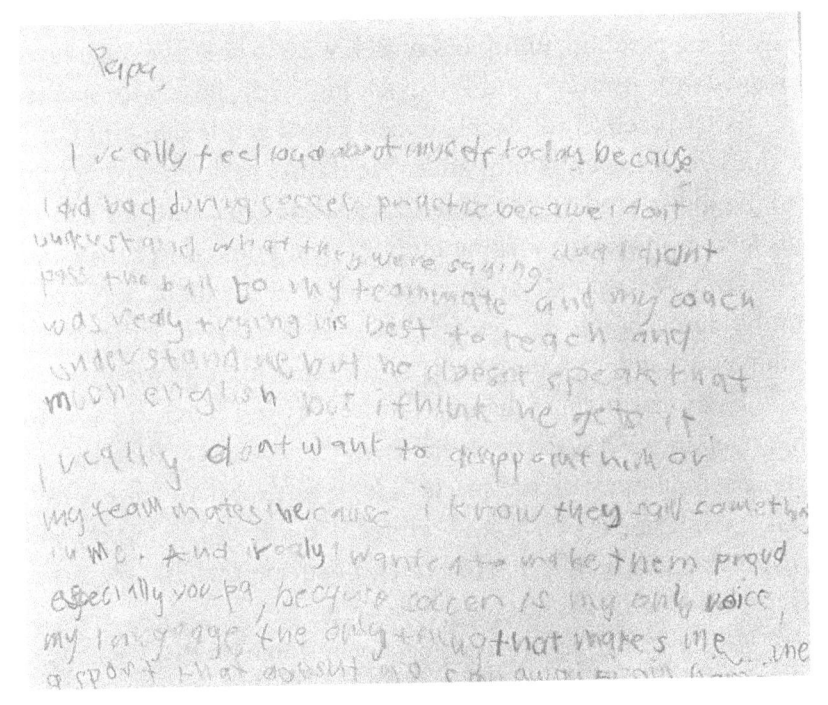

> Papa,
>
> I really feel bad about myself today because I did bad during soccer practice because I don't understand what they were saying, and I didn't pass the ball to my teammate and my coach was really trying his best to teach and understand me but he doesn't speak that much english but I think he gets it. I really don't want to disappoint him or my teammates because I know they all count on me. And I really want to make them proud especially you pa, because soccer is my only voice, my language, the only thing that makes me the sport that doesn't...

For Ethan, the language barrier hit hardest on the playground. School, which had once been a place of ease and familiarity, now felt like an alien world where he constantly tripped over his own words. The kids weren't unkind, but their chatter moved too quickly, their jokes too layered in cultural references for him to keep up. It was like watching a movie with the sound turned off, the action playing out in front of him while he missed the punchlines.

One afternoon, during soccer practice, Ethan found himself standing awkwardly by the sidelines. The other kids shouted directions in Tagalog, moving seamlessly around him. He wanted to join in, but every time he opened his mouth to speak, the words came out wrong. The embarrassment was a knot in his stomach that only tightened as the day wore on.

"Pass the ball!" one of the boys yelled, his voice barely discernible over the noise of the game.

Ethan hesitated, unsure of what had been said. He froze, the ball rolling past him, unnoticed until it was too late. The other boys groaned in frustration, and Ethan felt his cheeks flush with shame.

After practice, the coach, a man with a gentle demeanor and a thick accent, pulled him aside. He didn't speak much English, but he didn't need to. He patted Ethan's shoulder and gestured to his feet, mimicking a kicking motion, then pointed to Ethan and smiled. It was a simple gesture, but Ethan understood. The coach wasn't upset; he was encouraging him to keep trying. That small moment of understanding between them felt like a victory.

Later that night, Ethan sat down to write a letter to Papa. In his carefully scribbled words, he recounted the day's struggles but also the moment with the coach. "He doesn't speak much English, but I think he gets it," Ethan wrote. "He knows I'm trying, and that makes me feel like maybe I can get better at this. It's like soccer is its own language. I just have to learn it."

Allison's struggles with language were different. Being younger, she didn't have the same self-consciousness as Ethan or the weight of professional pressures like Asher. But her world was still full of confusion. She was learning the language in bits and pieces, picking up words from her classmates and her teacher, but it still wasn't enough. Some days, she felt like she was speaking through a thick glass wall, where her words couldn't quite reach the other side.

One afternoon, Allison found herself in a small, awkward circle of classmates during recess. They were talking animatedly about something—she wasn't sure what—but the excitement in their voices drew her in. She wanted to join, wanted to be part of the group. She tried to say something, offering a word she had learned the day before. But instead of responding, the kids burst into laughter.

Letters From The Heart

Her heart sank.

One of the girls, a kind-looking classmate named Lila, noticed Allison's distress and stepped forward. "It's okay," she said softly in broken English. "You said the word wrong. But it's okay, we learn together."

Allison blinked in surprise, the kindness unexpected. Lila gently corrected her, teaching her the right word and helping her say it properly. The other kids, seeing Allison's effort, stopped laughing and smiled instead. It was a small moment, but it was the first time Allison felt like maybe, just maybe, she could belong here.

That night, she wrote a letter to Papa about Lila. "I think I made a friend today," she wrote, her handwriting neat but tentative. "She's helping me with the words I don't know. Maybe it won't be so hard if I have someone to help me."

The language barrier wasn't just about words—it was about everything they didn't know. The unspoken rules, the customs, the tiny, intricate details that made life in the Philippines so different from what they had left behind. Asher knew this as well as anyone. He struggled in meetings, Ethan struggled on the playground, and Allison struggled in class. But slowly, through these moments of confusion and misunderstanding, they began to see that language wasn't just about words. It was about connection. It was about empathy.

As Asher reflected on these experiences, he began to see the parallels between their struggles with language and their emotional healing. Just as they stumbled through unfamiliar phrases, they were also stumbling through the process of rebuilding their lives. It wasn't always easy to find the right words—whether in Tagalog or in their own hearts—but every misstep, every mistake, was a part of the journey.

In a letter to Ethan and Allison, Asher wrote about this realization. "Learning a new language isn't just about getting the words right," he wrote. "It's about understanding each other, even when the words are hard to find. Just like we're learning to speak Tagalog, we're also learning to speak to each other about what we're going through. We'll make mistakes, but that's how we'll grow."

For Ethan, this message hit home. He had been struggling to open up to Papa about how lost he felt, not just in school but in his own head. But reading those words made him realize that maybe it was okay to struggle. Maybe it was okay not to have all the answers. Slowly, Ethan started to talk to Papa more—about school, about the kids who made him feel small, and about the moments when he felt like he was starting to understand this new world a little better.

Allison, too, began to open up. In her letters, she started to share more about her experiences at school, about the friends she was slowly making and the words she was learning. And as she did, the weight she had been carrying—the homesickness, the confusion—started to lighten, if only a little.

Over time, the family's struggles with language became less about the frustration of not understanding and more about the joy of learning together. Asher, Ethan, and Allison began to celebrate the small victories—the first time Ethan told a joke in Tagalog and the kids laughed with him, the moment Allison introduced herself to a new classmate without stumbling over her words, the day Asher navigated a work meeting without feeling lost.

Through it all, they learned that language was more than just words—it was connection, it was understanding, and it was patience. And as they grew more fluent in this new place, they also grew closer to each other, learning that the most important things—love, empathy, and resilience—didn't need translation. They were universal.

And with each word learned, with each connection made, they weren't just learning a new language—they were learning how to rebuild their family, one step, one word, at a time.

LONELINESS AND THE SEARCH FOR CONNECTION

In the stillness of their new home, between the hours of unpacking boxes and trying to make sense of their new surroundings, loneliness settled in like an unwelcome guest. Asher, Ethan, and Allison were each grappling with an overwhelming sense of isolation that had grown louder with every passing day. Manila was alive with people, noise, and chaos, yet somehow, they each felt more alone than ever before. The familiar routines, the comforting faces of friends and neighbors, the places they had known like the back of their hand—those had all been left behind in California, replaced by unfamiliar streets and foreign customs. The disconnection was palpable.

Asher, as the father, felt the weight of it most. He had always been the anchor of the family, the one who kept things moving forward even when the world felt shaky beneath their feet. But now, in this new country, he was adrift. His letters to Ethan and Allison were filled with encouragement, with reminders of how strong they were, how this new beginning would eventually feel like home. He masked his own loneliness behind these words, carefully hiding the fact that he, too, felt lost. He wanted to protect them from the harshness of the truth: that even he, their father, was struggling to find connection in a place where he felt like a perpetual outsider.

During his first few weeks at work, Asher did his best to engage with his colleagues. He made small talk, learned the names of everyone in the office, and even asked Mateo, his closest work friend, to explain some of the local customs that baffled him. But despite his efforts, every interaction felt surface-level, like he was skimming the edges of something deeper but never quite breaking through. The laughter he heard between colleagues, the easy flow of conversations in the breakroom, and the casual after-work drinks they invited each other to—it all felt like it belonged to a world he wasn't a part of.

He wrote to Ethan and Allison about the little victories, trying to stay positive. "I'm learning," he wrote, "about how things work here. It's different, but I think I'm getting the hang of it." He told them about the local dishes his coworkers brought in to share, about how he was slowly understanding more of the Tagalog spoken around him. But what he didn't tell them was how, even in the middle of a bustling office, he had never felt more isolated. He longed for the comfort of familiarity, for conversations that didn't feel like a balancing act of trying not to offend, not to misunderstand, not to reveal too much of his inner uncertainty.

For Ethan and Allison, school was a different kind of battleground. Their loneliness came in waves, crashing over them at the most unexpected moments.

Ethan, always the more introspective of the two, felt the weight of being the "new kid" at school more intensely than he had anticipated. His journal entries were filled with frustration, confusion, and a growing sense of disconnection. It wasn't just the language barrier, though that was a significant part of it. It was the way the other kids seemed to effortlessly fit into their groups, laughing and talking about things he didn't understand. He tried to join in, but his words always came out wrong. Every attempt to make friends felt clumsy and awkward, and after a while, he stopped trying.

"I sit in class, surrounded by people, and yet I feel invisible," he wrote in one particularly raw journal entry. "They talk to each other, and I watch, but I don't know how to join in. I miss my friends back home. I miss being known."

For Allison, the loneliness took on a softer, more bittersweet tone. At seven years old, she didn't have the same understanding of why things were so hard, but she felt it all the same. Her letters to Papa and Ethan were filled with memories of her old life—of playing with her best friend, Sarah, during recess, of the way their old house smelled like Mama's cooking, of the neighborhood cat she used to feed after school. She missed the familiarity of everything. The new school was loud and confusing, and while the kids were nice enough, none of them felt like her friends. They didn't know her favorite game, or the way she loved to draw when she was feeling sad.

"I ate lunch alone today," Allison wrote in a letter to Papa, her handwriting neat and small. "It's not so bad. I like the food here, but I miss Sarah. I miss having someone to talk to."

The loneliness in her words cut through Asher's heart like a knife. He hated knowing that his children were struggling, and there was so little he could do to fix it. He wrote back to both of them, pouring love and encouragement into his letters. "You're both so strong," he reminded them. "Making friends takes time, but you'll get there. Don't give up."

But even as he wrote those words, Asher knew how hollow they must have sounded. Because deep down, he was grappling with the same fears—what if they never found their place here? What if this sense of being adrift never went away?

But as the weeks passed, something started to shift. The overwhelming loneliness didn't disappear, but it began to loosen its grip on their hearts, just a little.

It started with small, almost imperceptible moments.

One afternoon, while Asher was heading back to the apartment after a long day of work, his neighbor, Mrs. Reyes, waved him over from her porch. She was a warm, elderly woman who had lived in the building for decades. Her smile was inviting, and Asher had spoken to her in passing before, but this time, she invited him inside.

"Come, sit," she said, her voice rich with the lilt of Tagalog. "You're new here, yes? Let me tell you about our neighborhood. There's a festival this weekend—you and your children should come."

Asher hesitated for a moment, unsure of what to say. He had never been one to join in local events, especially since he didn't feel fully integrated yet. But something about Mrs. Reyes' kindness made him nod in agreement. "Thank you," he said, smiling. "That sounds great."

The local festival turned out to be a turning point. The streets were alive with music, laughter, and the smells of sizzling food from vendors lining the sidewalks. For the first time in months, Asher felt like he was a part of something larger than himself, like the community was slowly opening its doors to him and his children.

Ethan, too, found his own small victory. His soccer coach had been patient with him, helping him ease into the team despite the language barrier. At first, Ethan felt like an outsider, the kids speaking too quickly for him to follow, the drills confusing in their unfamiliarity. But one day, after weeks of practice, Ethan scored a goal during a scrimmage. The boys on his team cheered, patting him on the back, and for the first time, Ethan felt like he belonged.

"It was like I didn't need to speak the same language," Ethan wrote in his journal. "The cheers said everything. I'm not just the new kid anymore. I'm part of the team."

Allison's journey toward connection came through an unexpected friendship with a classmate named Lila. They had been paired together for an art project, and at first, Allison was shy, unsure of how to start a conversation. But Lila was patient, guiding Allison through the assignment and complimenting her drawings. The two girls bonded over their love of art, and soon, they were spending recess together, coloring and sharing stories about their families.

"I think I have a new friend," Allison wrote to Papa. "She's really nice, and she likes to draw, just like me. Maybe this school isn't so bad after all."

Asher's letters to his children started to reflect a new tone. Instead of simply offering encouragement, he began sharing his own experiences of connection. He wrote about Mrs. Reyes and how her invitation had made him feel like a part of the neighborhood. He told them about his coworkers, how he was slowly learning their jokes and joining in on conversations. "It's funny," he wrote, "how one small gesture can make you feel like you belong. I think we're all finding our place here, little by little."

Ethan and Allison's journals mirrored this shift. Ethan wrote with more confidence, describing his growing bond with his soccer team. "It's not as hard as it used to be," he wrote. "I still don't understand everything, but I don't feel like an outsider anymore." Allison's entries blossomed with hope, her words reflecting the joy of friendship. "Lila and I are going to work on another project together," she wrote excitedly. "Maybe we can play after school one day!"

The family's journey toward connection wasn't without setbacks. There were still days when the loneliness crept back in—days when Asher felt the weight of being an outsider at work, when Ethan struggled to understand a conversation, or when Allison missed her old friends so much that it hurt. But those days were becoming fewer, replaced by moments of connection that slowly began to weave themselves into the fabric of their lives.

One evening, as the three of them sat around the dinner table, eating a meal Asher had learned to cook from Mrs. Reyes, he looked at his children and felt a sense of peace wash over him. They were laughing—real, genuine laughter—and for the first time since their move, the sound didn't feel foreign. It felt like home.

"I'm proud of you both," Asher said, his voice soft but filled with emotion. "I know this hasn't been easy, but look how far we've come." Ethan smiled, his usual quiet demeanor giving way to a rare moment of openness. "Yeah," he said, glancing at Allison. "We're getting there."

Allison beamed, her face lighting up with the joy of the moment. "I like it here," she said simply. "I think... I think this could be home."

Asher's heart swelled with pride and relief. They weren't just surviving anymore. They were living. They were connecting. They were finding their place.

In the months that followed, the sense of loneliness that had once felt suffocating began to fade. The family continued to write letters and journal entries, but the tone had shifted. There was still uncertainty, still moments of homesickness, but now there was also hope, connection, and the promise of new beginnings.

Asher's letters to his children no longer masked his own struggles. Instead, they celebrated their shared victories—the neighbors who waved to them each morning, the friendships that had blossomed, the way the city was slowly becoming their own. Ethan's journal entries spoke of camaraderie with his teammates, the joy of understanding a new language, and the pride he felt in being part of something bigger. Allison's letters were filled with stories of her and Lila, of art projects and after-school games, of the comfort that came with having a friend to share her days with.

Loneliness had once been their greatest challenge, but now, it was merely a memory, something they had faced and overcome together. The ache of isolation had been replaced by the warmth of connection, and while their new life wasn't perfect, it was theirs.

Together, they had learned that loneliness, though formidable, wasn't invincible. The human spirit's resilience, the capacity for forming new bonds, and the willingness to keep trying had carried them through the hardest days. And now, as they sat around the dinner table, laughing together, they knew they had found something that would carry them through whatever challenges lay ahead: each other.

CHAPTER 4

PART III: ECHOES OF THE PAST

Asher's Reflections on Marriage and Divorce

As I sit here, pen in hand, trying to capture the swirling thoughts that have occupied my mind for so long, I'm confronted by the emotional storm that surrounds my marriage and its ultimate collapse. The decision to walk away from a relationship that had once been my anchor, my home, wasn't made on a whim. It was a choice born out of long, sleepless nights, quiet moments of doubt, and, eventually, the painful realization that love, on its own, is not always enough. The dissolution of my marriage wasn't just an ending—it was a reckoning. A reckoning with who I had become and who I needed to be, both for myself and for my children.

Marriage, in the beginning, feels like a promise that will never fade. I remember our wedding day as if it were yesterday—the bright eyes of my bride, the nervous excitement in my chest, the certainty that we could weather any storm as long as we faced it together. But storms don't always come with thunder and lightning. Sometimes they arrive in silence, creeping in over years, eroding the foundation slowly, until one day, you wake up and realize you're standing on broken ground. That's what happened to us. There wasn't one defining moment that shattered our bond, no one explosive argument or betrayal. It was a gradual unraveling, the kind that happens when life pulls you in different directions and you lose sight of each other along the way.

Now, looking back, I can't pinpoint the exact moment things shifted. Maybe it was when the kids came along and we got so wrapped up in being parents that we forgot how to be partners. Or maybe it was when the daily grind of life—the bills, the jobs, the exhaustion—wore us down to the point where we had nothing left to give each other. Whatever the reason, the result was the same: a growing distance that neither of us knew how to bridge.

There were times when I wondered if we could have saved it. If we had tried harder, communicated better, or fought for it with more intensity. Those are the thoughts that still linger in the quiet moments—the 'what ifs' that haunt me late at night. But as much as I want to hold on to those memories of what we once were, I also know that clinging to the past isn't the answer. Our marriage ended because it had to. It ended because staying together, despite the love that still flickered between us, was slowly extinguishing who we both were.

I've learned that divorce, as painful and heartbreaking as it is, can also be a catalyst for growth. It forces you to confront parts of yourself that you'd rather keep hidden. In the aftermath of the separation, I had to face my own shortcomings, my own failures as a husband. I realized that I had placed so much of my identity in being a provider, in making sure the bills were paid and the house was stable, that I had neglected the emotional work of marriage. I had stopped being present, stopped listening, stopped showing up in the ways that truly mattered. Divorce ripped that bandage off, forcing me to take a hard look at who I was and who I needed to become.

One of the hardest lessons I've had to learn is that the end of a marriage doesn't equate to the end of a family. It's easy to feel like divorce means failure, that it means you've somehow broken the very thing that was supposed to last forever. But I've come to understand that family can be redefined. It's not about two parents under one roof—it's about the love, support, and connection we maintain, even if the structure looks different. Ethan and Allison are still my world, and I am still theirs. Our family hasn't been destroyed; it's just evolved into something new. And while that evolution has been painful, it's also been necessary.

In this new chapter, I'm trying to be a different kind of father. Not just the provider, but the listener. The one who shows up not just with solutions, but with empathy and understanding. Divorce has taught me that emotional presence is more important than any material thing I could offer them. The letters we exchange have become our lifeline. In those letters, I see not just their struggles, but their resilience. And in writing back to them, I'm reminded of my own strength—of the commitment I made to be the best father I can be, despite the mistakes I've made along the way.

I remember one of the first letters Ethan wrote to me after the move. It wasn't long, but it was raw and honest in a way that cut me to the core. He told me how much he missed home, how lonely he felt, how hard it was to navigate this new life. And in the middle of that letter, he asked a question that I wasn't ready to answer: "Papa, why did everything have to change?" In that moment, I realized that my children were not just adjusting to a new country—they were also grappling with the aftershocks of our divorce. Their world had been split in two, just like mine. And they were looking to me to make sense of it all.

I didn't have an easy answer for him. How could I? How do you explain to a thirteen-year-old that sometimes love isn't enough, that sometimes the person you thought you'd spend forever with just isn't your forever after all? Instead of giving him a neatly wrapped explanation, I chose honesty. I told him that I didn't have all the answers, but that I was doing my best to make sure we were okay, that we were building something new together. And that's been my approach ever since—honesty, even when it's hard. Honesty, even when it hurts. Because I've come to believe that honesty is the foundation of healing. It's what will allow us to rebuild trust and to create a new kind of stability, even in the midst of all this change.

In reflecting on the end of my marriage, I've realized that the pain, while ever-present, is no longer all-consuming. There's a strange kind of relief that comes with accepting the end of something that wasn't working anymore. It's not the relief of being free from responsibility—because I'm still responsible for Ethan, for Allison, for making sure they know they're loved and supported. It's more like the relief of knowing that we've been given a second chance to build something better, something healthier, even if it looks different from what I once imagined.

Divorce has been a crucible for personal growth, for all of us. It's forced me to reevaluate my priorities and to look closely at the kind of father I want to be. I've had to let go of the idea that a perfect family means two parents together under one roof. A perfect family, I've learned, is one where love is constant, even if the structure has changed. It's one where the kids know they're safe, supported, and understood. I want Ethan and Allison to know that no matter what, we are still a family. That hasn't changed.

As I write this, I'm reminded of a moment that occurred shortly after the divorce was finalized. Ethan, who had been withdrawn and sullen for weeks, finally opened up. He asked me if I was still angry with Mama. It was a question that caught me off guard, but I knew I had to be careful with my response. After a long pause, I told him the truth: "No, I'm not angry. I'm sad that things didn't work out, but I'm not angry anymore." He nodded, and I could see the weight of that answer lift something off his shoulders. He needed to know that while our family had changed, the love and respect I had for his mother remained intact. He needed to see that even in the midst of heartache, we could still move forward with kindness.

Allison, being younger, hasn't asked as many direct questions, but I see the way she looks at me when she thinks I'm not paying attention. She's watching, observing how I handle the aftermath of the divorce. She's learning, just like Ethan, what it means to face hardship and come out the other side. I want her to know that it's okay to feel all of these emotions—to be sad, angry, confused—but that those feelings don't have to define her. They don't have to define any of us.

Through all of this, I've come to realize that our journey isn't just about healing from the divorce. It's about rediscovering who we are as individuals and as a family. It's about learning to love each other in new ways, to communicate more openly, and to support each other through the highs and lows. The end of my marriage was not the end of our story—it was the beginning of a new chapter. A chapter that's messy, complicated, and full of unknowns, but also one that holds the promise of growth and healing.

I used to think that divorce was synonymous with failure. That if a marriage ended, it meant you had somehow failed as a partner, as a parent, as a person. But I don't believe that anymore. I've learned that sometimes, the bravest thing you can do is let go of something that isn't serving you anymore. Sometimes, the greatest act of love is allowing yourself and the people you care about to find happiness in a different way.

As I look forward, I'm filled with a sense of cautious optimism. I don't know exactly what the future holds for us, but I do know that we'll face it together. Ethan, Allison, and I—we're building something new. It's not perfect, and it never will be, but it's ours. And in that, I find hope.

Hope that we can continue to heal, to grow, and to redefine what family means for us. Because even after everything, we are still bound by love—and that, more than anything, is what will carry us forward.

ETHAN'S ANGER AND CONFUSION

Ethan had always been the quiet one, the kid who kept his emotions bottled up, his thoughts neatly organized in the back of his mind. But in the weeks following the divorce, everything he had kept locked away came crashing to the surface. The letter he wrote to his father that day was not a carefully constructed piece of writing; it was a storm of raw, untamed emotion. The thirteen-year-old's usual tidy handwriting now sprawled across the page in jagged, uneven lines, as if the words were too wild to be contained. Each word reflected the turmoil inside his heart, each stroke of the pen a testament to the chaos he felt.

> I don't understand you pa, I don't understand, everything that you do? Was it my fault? that everything didn't worked out for us was it because of me? If it wasn't there will everything be different. Why pa! Why the sudden change of heart for you and mama. I was often called as someone whos parents got divorce, a parentless child. How could mama

"Why did you leave us, Mama?" he scrawled, his frustration practically tearing through the paper. "How could you just walk away from our family? From me and Allison? It's not fair!"

His anger, confusion, and grief exploded onto the page, questions he didn't even know how to fully articulate swirling in his mind. For Ethan, the divorce was a tidal wave that had swept through their lives, leaving behind wreckage that didn't make any sense. The home he had known, the life he had grown comfortable in—it was all gone, ripped away without warning. And all he was left with were questions, unanswered and hanging in the air, suffocating him.

As Asher sat on the edge of his bed, reading his son's letter, the words blurred through the tears welling up in his eyes. The weight of Ethan's pain settled like a stone in his chest. Asher had expected anger, had known this day would come, but seeing it on the page, so raw and unfiltered, tore at him in a way nothing else had. His heart ached for his son, for the confusion and betrayal Ethan must have felt. Asher recognized these feelings too well—the same anger and bewilderment he had harbored as a boy when his own parents had separated. It was like looking in a mirror and seeing his younger self reflected in Ethan's hurt.

"I don't understand," Ethan had written. "How can you and Mama not fix this? Why did it have to end like this? Don't you care about us anymore?"

Asher could feel the unspoken question buried beneath Ethan's words: Was it my fault? He knew that behind all of Ethan's anger, there was fear and self-doubt. Divorce, to a child, often felt like rejection, a shattering of the very foundation on which their sense of safety and belonging was built. Ethan, at thirteen, was caught between wanting to understand and being too young to fully grasp the complexities of his parents' choices.

Asher sat in silence for what felt like hours, the letter clutched in his hands, his heart heavy. He knew that he couldn't leave these words unanswered. His son needed him now more than ever, and how he responded to Ethan's anger could set the tone for their future relationship. But how could he explain something so complex, something that even adults struggled to understand? How could he tell his son that, sometimes, love alone isn't enough?

Ethan's frustration had been building for weeks. At school, he felt like he didn't fit anywhere. He was "the kid whose parents got divorced," a label he despised but couldn't shake. His teachers offered sympathetic glances, his friends didn't know what to say, and he hated every second of it. He didn't want pity. He wanted his life back. He wanted his family to be whole again, for everything to go back to the way it was before the separation shattered his world.

He found himself lashing out in small ways. He was short with Allison, who asked too many questions he didn't know how to answer. He was distant with his father, who he blamed for not fighting harder, for not doing whatever it took to keep the family together. And his anger at his mother? That burned the hottest of all. How could she just leave? Didn't she care about him? Didn't she care about Allison? These thoughts circled his mind constantly, fueling his resentment.

At night, when the house was quiet and everyone else was asleep, Ethan would lie awake, staring at the ceiling, replaying every argument, every cold silence between his parents in the months leading up to the divorce. He didn't have all the details, but he could piece together enough to understand that something had broken between them. And as much as he tried to ignore it, deep down, he wondered if he had something to do with it.

Asher knew that he had to respond to Ethan's letter, but he couldn't rush it. He needed to get it right. So, late one night, he sat at the kitchen table, a cup of cold coffee in front of him, staring at the blank piece of paper before him. He wanted to be honest with Ethan—his son deserved that much—but he also knew he had to be careful with his words. Ethan's world was fragile right now, and Asher didn't want to cause any more cracks in its foundation.

He began writing slowly, his pen hovering over the paper as he searched for the right words.

"Ethan," he wrote, "I hear your anger, and I understand your confusion. I know how much pain you're feeling right now, and I'm so sorry that you have to go through this. I wish I could take that pain away, but I can't. What I can do is be here for you. I'm always here to listen, to answer your questions, to help you make sense of everything—even when I don't have all the answers myself."

He paused, his thoughts racing, and then continued.

"The decision to separate was incredibly difficult, and it wasn't made lightly. I know it seems like something that should have been easy to fix, but sometimes, even when two people love each other, they can't make things work the way they used to. Your mother and I did everything we could to try and stay together, but in the end, we realized that separating was the best thing for all of us, even if it doesn't feel that way right now."

Asher's hand trembled as he wrote the next part, knowing how crucial it was.

"I want you to know, Ethan, that none of this is your fault. The problems between your mother and me were ours to deal with, and no matter what happens between us, my love for you and Allison will never change. You're both the most important parts of my life, and I will always be here for you, no matter what. This family is different now, but it's still a family. We're still a family."

He read over the words, unsure if they were enough but hoping they would be a start. As he sealed the letter, Asher hoped that his honesty would help Ethan begin to navigate the emotional storm he was trapped in. It wasn't a perfect answer, but it was the best he could offer—a bridge, however fragile, back to his son.

Days passed, and though Asher gave Ethan space, he noticed the subtle changes in his son's demeanor. Ethan was quieter than usual, more withdrawn. He still came to soccer practice, still played video games with Allison, but there was an emotional distance that hadn't been there before the divorce.

One evening, Asher sat down next to Ethan on the couch, careful not to push too hard. "How are you doing, bud?" he asked, trying to sound casual but knowing the conversation they both needed to have was anything but.

Ethan shrugged, eyes fixed on the TV. "I don't know," he muttered, the frustration evident in his tone. "I'm just... mad, I guess."

Asher nodded, feeling his heart clench. "That's okay," he said softly. "You're allowed to be mad. I'm mad too sometimes."

That caught Ethan's attention. He looked at his father, surprised. "You are?"

"Yeah," Asher admitted. "This isn't what I wanted either, Ethan. I wanted our family to stay together, to make things work. But sometimes... life doesn't go the way we plan. And it's okay to be upset about that."

Ethan looked away, his jaw clenched, but Asher could see the emotion behind his eyes. "I just... don't get it," Ethan finally said, his voice breaking slightly. "Why did everything have to change? Why couldn't you and Mama just... fix it?"

Asher took a deep breath, feeling the weight of the conversation pressing down on him. "I wish it were that simple," he said gently. "But sometimes, even when two people love each other, they grow apart. Your mother and I both tried, but staying together would have hurt all of us more in the long run. It's hard to understand, but I promise you, we made the decision because we thought it was what was best for everyone."

For a long moment, Ethan didn't say anything. Asher wondered if he had pushed too far, if maybe he should have left it alone. But then, Ethan spoke, his voice quieter now. "I just... miss how things used to be."

"I miss it too," Asher said, his own voice thick with emotion. "But we're still a family, Ethan. That hasn't changed."

Ethan looked at him then, and for the first time in weeks, Asher saw a flicker of understanding in his son's eyes. It wasn't a resolution—it would take time for that—but it was a step. And for now, that was enough.

> Papa,
>
> I dont understand you
> pa I felt to recognize you at all.
> I thought that I was the only one struggling
> and missed home but after knowing how
> you felt. I guess its a good thing and it
> helps that i am not the only one. the
> only one who looks back at the
> memories we had back at Cali

As Asher watched his son turn back to the TV, he felt a small sense of relief. They had a long road ahead of them, but they would walk it together, one step at a time. Ethan's anger and confusion weren't gone, but Asher knew that with patience, honesty, and love, they would find their way through the storm.

And as he sat there beside his son, he felt the tiniest spark of hope—hope that, despite everything, they would come out the other side stronger than before.

ALLISON'S QUEST FOR IDENTITY

In the swirl of unfamiliar faces, new sounds, and foreign streets, Allison found herself standing on the precipice of two worlds. She was no longer just the little girl from California, the one who knew her place in the comfortable rhythm of American life. Now, she was something else, something in between. The move to the Philippines had not only changed her surroundings, but it also had triggered questions she didn't know how to answer: Who am I now?

At seven years old, Allison had always been curious, asking questions about everything from why the sky was blue to how birds knew when to fly south. But now, her curiosity had taken on a different weight. Her letters to her father were filled with more than just stories of her day—they carried the complex emotions of a child trying to reconcile the world she had left behind with the new one she found herself in.

"Papa," she wrote one afternoon, her pencil pressing heavily against the paper, "I feel like I don't fit here. Everyone talks differently, and I don't understand all the words. At school, the kids are nice, but they talk about things I've never heard of. I try to listen, but it's hard to know what to say."

She paused, looking out the window at the city below. Manila was loud and alive, nothing like the quiet suburban streets of Los Angeles. Sometimes, the noise made her feel small, like she was being swallowed up by a place too big for her to understand. And yet, there was something about the city that fascinated her. The streets buzzed with activity, vendors selling fruit she had never tasted, tricycles zipping by, and street performers playing music that floated through the air. It was different, yes, but it was also... exciting.

That excitement was tempered by the confusion she felt at school, where she was "the new kid," the girl with the accent, the one who didn't always understand the conversations around her. Even the simplest tasks, like saying "hello" or "thank you," felt complicated when the words didn't come out the way they were supposed to. Her classmates would giggle when she mispronounced a word in Tagalog, not out of malice, but out of the kind of innocent amusement children have when something doesn't quite fit. Allison's cheeks would burn with embarrassment, but she forced herself to smile along with them.

In her letters to Ethan, she shared more of her frustrations.

"I tried to ask my teacher for another pencil today, but I said it wrong again," she wrote one day. "Everyone laughed, and I know they didn't mean to hurt my feelings, but it still felt bad. Why can't I just say the words right? Why is everything here so hard?"

Ethan, older and more reserved, often responded with encouragement. "You'll get it," he wrote back. "It's just going to take time. And remember, they're not laughing at you. They just think it's funny because it's different. You're learning something new. That's not easy."

But amidst the confusion, there were also small victories. Allison was determined to learn, to fit in, to find her place in this strange new world. Her father had enrolled her in a language class, and slowly, she began picking up words and phrases. Each time she mastered a new word, she would practice it over and over until it felt right in her mouth. And when she got it right—when the word flowed smoothly and her classmates smiled instead of laughed—it felt like she had conquered a small mountain.

One day, she came home beaming. "Papa, I did it! I asked for a pencil in Tagalog, and no one laughed. I said it right!"

Her father smiled, pulling her into a hug. "That's wonderful, sweetheart. See? You're getting better every day."

These small victories began to add up. Allison made her first friend, a girl named Lila who loved to draw as much as Allison did. They spent recess sitting together under a tree, sketching pictures of their favorite animals and talking about school. Lila patiently helped Allison with her Tagalog, and in return, Allison taught her a few English words. It was the first time Allison felt like she was building a bridge between the two worlds she inhabited.

In one of her letters to Ethan, she excitedly shared the news: "Lila says I'm getting really good at drawing! We drew a whole jungle today with monkeys and parrots. And she helped me with some words I didn't know. I think we're going to be best friends."

But the journey wasn't without its bumps. As Allison became more comfortable with Filipino customs and language, she found herself feeling conflicted. On the one hand, she was proud of her progress, proud of the fact that she was beginning to understand the world around her. On the other hand, she worried she was losing touch with the girl she used to be—the American girl who loved pancakes for breakfast and knew all the words to her favorite cartoons.

"Papa," she wrote one evening, "I like it here, I really do. But sometimes, I feel like I'm forgetting things from home. Like, when I try to remember how Mama used to cook, it's hard to picture it. What if I start forgetting everything about who I was before we came here?"

Her father's response came a few days later, in a letter that felt more like a hug than anything else. "Allison, you're not losing who you are. You're adding to it. You're learning new things, and that's a good thing. You'll always be the same Allison—no matter where we are, no matter what you learn. Home is something you carry with you."

Those words stayed with Allison. She didn't have to choose between being American or Filipino. She could be both. She was both. The idea of embracing her dual identity began to take root in her heart. She started to see her experiences not as confusing contradictions, but as pieces of a larger puzzle that made her who she was.

Her fascination with Filipino culture deepened. At school, she joined a multicultural club, where students from different backgrounds shared their traditions. Allison proudly taught her classmates about American holidays like Thanksgiving and Halloween, and in return, she learned about Filipino customs—Pasko, the Christmas celebrations that lasted for months, and fiestas, community festivals full of food, music, and dancing. She marveled at how these two cultures, so different in many ways, could exist side by side within her.

One of her favorite memories was the first time she and her father cooked a traditional Filipino dish together. It had been a long day, and Papa suggested they make adobo, a savory chicken stew that their neighbors often raved about. As they chopped garlic and onions, stirring the pot while the delicious aroma filled the kitchen, Allison felt a connection—not just to the food, but to the culture she was slowly becoming a part of.

"Papa," she said, as they sat down to eat, "do you think Mama would like this?"

Her father smiled, a soft sadness in his eyes. "I think she would. And I think she'd be proud of you, Allison. You're learning so much."

Cooking together became a way for Allison to explore her Filipino roots while still holding on to the parts of her that were undeniably American. Some nights, they made burgers and fries; other nights, it was sinigang, a sour tamarind soup. Each meal was a blend of both cultures, just like her.

In her letters to Ethan, Allison began to talk more about this balance she was learning to strike.

"I think I get it now," she wrote. "I don't have to choose. I can be both. I can love my American shows and still celebrate Filipino holidays. I can speak English and Tagalog. I'm not stuck between two worlds—I'm lucky because I get to live in both."

Her brother's response was simple but heartfelt. "That's really cool, Allison. I'm proud of you."

By the end of her first year in the Philippines, Allison's journey of self-discovery had taken her to places she hadn't expected. She still missed her life in California, still missed her friends and the familiar comfort of home, but she no longer felt like she was losing herself. Instead, she realized she was growing into someone new— someone who could carry both parts of her identity with pride.

In her final letter to Ethan before the summer break, she reflected on the transformation she had undergone.

"I think I'm starting to understand who I am," she wrote. "It's like I'm two different pieces, but they fit together. I don't have to choose one or the other. I'm American, but I'm also Filipino. And I'm proud of both. I think that's what makes me... me."

Her words echoed a sentiment that so many children of immigrant families come to understand as they navigate the complex terrain of cultural identity. Allison's journey wasn't just about learning a new language or making friends—it was about finding a way to embrace all the pieces of who she was, even the ones that didn't seem to fit at first.

In the end, Allison's quest for identity became a testament to the power of resilience, self-acceptance, and the beauty of cultural fusion. She learned that identity isn't about choosing one path or the other—it's about weaving them together, creating something entirely new and uniquely hers.

And with that realization, Allison knew that no matter where life took her, she would always carry both parts of herself with her, woven together like the colors of a tapestry—strong, beautiful, and whole.

CHAPTER 5
PART IV: BUILDING BRIDGES

Finding Support in Unexpected Places

Life in the Philippines had been challenging for Asher, Ethan, and Allison—more challenging than any of them had expected. They had arrived with hope and determination, but the reality of starting over in a foreign land quickly set in. The move had stripped away their familiar routines, leaving them adrift in a sea of uncertainties. Yet, in the midst of these struggles, the family found support in the most unexpected places—encounters and friendships that would shape their new lives in ways they hadn't imagined.

Asher was the first to stumble upon this unexpected lifeline. One afternoon, while running errands, he passed by a local community center that caught his attention. The building was modest, with faded banners advertising workshops and events pinned to the walls. Asher, feeling the weight of single parenthood bearing down on him, walked in almost on a whim, curious about what it had to offer.

That's where he met Rosa.

Rosa was seated behind the reception desk, her warm smile immediately making Asher feel at ease. She introduced herself as a volunteer coordinator and asked if Asher was looking for something specific. He wasn't—at least, not until she mentioned the support group for single parents that met every Tuesday.

Asher hesitated. Support groups weren't his thing, and the idea of sitting in a circle with strangers talking about his problems didn't exactly appeal to him. But Rosa, sensing his reluctance, leaned in and said, "Sometimes, it helps to hear from people who understand. You don't have to do this alone."

There was something in her tone—an understanding, a quiet confidence—that made Asher stop and think. He had been carrying so much on his shoulders: trying to be strong for Ethan and Allison, figuring out how to co-parent with their mother from halfway across the world, navigating a new job in a new culture. Maybe he didn't have to carry it all by himself.

The following Tuesday, Asher found himself sitting in a circle with a dozen other parents, listening as they shared their stories. Some were navigating the complexities of divorce; others had lost their partners. As the sessions went on, Asher realized that it wasn't just about sharing the pain—it was about finding practical solutions too. Tips on managing finances, advice on co-parenting, and even recommendations on local schools or affordable babysitters flowed freely in the group.

For the first time since the divorce, Asher didn't feel so alone. These people understood the weight he carried, and slowly, he found himself opening up, sharing his struggles and fears. The group became more than just a meeting—it became a place where Asher could breathe, reflect, and gain strength. He even began to look forward to Tuesdays, where he would learn something new that helped him be a better father, a better version of himself.

Meanwhile, Ethan and Allison were having their own moments of unexpected support at school. At first, both had been wary of their new surroundings. Ethan had been dreading the cliques that came with middle school, and Allison had feared being the "new kid" in a place where she didn't know the language or the customs.

But life, as it often does, surprised them.

Ethan's first surprise came during P.E., of all places. He had always been decent at sports but hadn't expected to stand out in any way. That changed during a soccer game when, in a moment of pure adrenaline, he scored a goal that sent the ball flying past the goalie. His teammates, who had been indifferent toward him up until that point, erupted in cheers, patting him on the back and shouting, "Nice shot!" It wasn't just a lucky break—it was the beginning of something new.

After the game, one of the boys, Marco, came up to Ethan and said, "You're pretty good. We could use you on the team."

Ethan blinked in surprise. "The team?"

"Yeah, we play after school. You should join us."

And just like that, Ethan found himself being accepted in a way he hadn't expected. Soccer became his way in—a common ground that made the language barrier a little less daunting. On the field, it didn't matter that his Tagalog was shaky; what mattered was that he could keep up, that he was part of something. The awkward silences in class began to fade as the boys in his team welcomed him into their conversations. They taught him new phrases, corrected his mistakes without mocking him, and even invited him to their after-school hangouts.

For the first time in weeks, Ethan started to feel like he belonged.

Allison's experience was different, but no less heartening. One of her biggest fears was not being able to make friends. But that fear began to dissolve when her teacher, Mrs. Santos, introduced a new project in class. Each student was asked to share a piece of their culture with the class, and the diverse makeup of the students meant there were presentations about everything from traditional Filipino festivals to Malaysian food to Japanese calligraphy.

Allison had been nervous about her turn, unsure if anyone would care about the American traditions she missed so much. But when she got up in front of the class and started talking about

Thanksgiving—complete with pictures of turkey dinners and descriptions of how her family used to watch the Macy's Thanksgiving Day Parade—her classmates were captivated.

"That's so cool!" one girl exclaimed. "You have a parade every year?"

Another boy chimed in, asking if they really ate pumpkin pie like the cartoons showed.

Allison, thrilled by their interest, nodded eagerly. "Yeah! My papa makes the best one."

From that day forward, Allison no longer felt like an outsider. The class became curious about her culture, asking questions and sharing their own traditions with her in return. She and her classmates would spend lunch trading stories about their families, laughing over the differences and marveling at the similarities. Allison began to understand that being different wasn't something to be ashamed of—it was something to be proud of. It made her interesting; it made her Allison.

Then there was Mrs. Erin Connelly, their elderly neighbor, who had been quietly watching the family's struggles since the day they moved in. Mrs. Erin Connelly had been an immigrant herself once, though many years ago. She understood the challenges of adapting to a new country, the loneliness, and the sense of displacement. But she also knew the strength that came from pushing through those hardships.

One afternoon, Asher came home from work to find Mrs. Erin Connelly standing outside her door, holding a basket filled with food. "I made some adobo," she said with a soft smile. "Thought you and the kids might like a home-cooked meal."

Asher, exhausted and grateful, invited her in, and that meal became the first of many shared moments with their neighbor. Mrs. Erin Connelly quickly became a fixture in their lives, her wisdom and warmth filling a gap that Asher hadn't realized existed. She shared stories of her own journey to the Philippines decades ago, stories of survival, of resilience, and of finding joy in the little things.

"Home isn't always where you come from," she told Allison one evening, after the girl had asked her how she had adjusted to life as an immigrant. "Home is where you build it. And right now, you're building yours. It will take time, but you'll find that one day, this place will feel like it's always been home."

Mrs. Erin Connelly's quiet wisdom resonated with all of them. She didn't try to solve their problems or offer easy answers. Instead, she gave them the space to figure things out on their own, gently guiding them along the way. Her presence was like a steadying hand, reassuring them that they weren't alone—that others had walked this path before and come out stronger on the other side.

Slowly but surely, life began to take shape in ways that none of them had anticipated. Asher found his rhythm through the support group, his Tuesday meetings becoming a space where he could share, vent, and heal alongside people who understood the complexities of single parenthood. Ethan's place in his soccer team gave him a sense of belonging, a reminder that being the new kid didn't have to mean being an outsider forever. And Allison, with her newfound friends and the wisdom of Mrs. Erin Connelly, began to see herself as someone who wasn't torn between two cultures, but who was lucky enough to embrace both.

The family's journey was far from over—there were still challenges ahead, moments of homesickness and confusion that would rear their heads when they least expected it. But for the first time in a long while, they didn't feel like they were simply surviving. They were living. They were building something new, something that blended the best parts of their old life with the richness of their new one.

And as they sat around the dinner table one evening, sharing a meal that was a fusion of American and Filipino dishes—Ethan's favorite mac and cheese alongside Allison's new obsession, lumpia—they laughed and talked with an ease that had been missing for months.

In the end, they had found support in places they never would have expected: in a community center, on a soccer field, in a multicultural classroom, and in the gentle presence of an elderly neighbor. It was a reminder that family wasn't just about blood—it was about the people who showed up when you needed them most, the ones who helped you navigate the hardest parts of life and made you feel like you belonged, even when you were far from home.

THE POWER OF VULNERABILITY

In the months following their move, Asher, Ethan, and Allison learned that healing after a divorce wasn't just about finding new routines or adjusting to life in a different country—it was about letting themselves feel. Vulnerability, something Asher had long avoided, became an unexpected ally in their journey. Through their letters, journal entries, and quiet conversations, they discovered that opening up about their fears, insecurities, and hopes wasn't a sign of weakness. It was a powerful tool for connection, growth, and ultimately, healing.

Asher had always been the strong one. After the divorce, he believed his role as a father meant shielding Ethan and Allison from the full weight of his emotions. He needed to be their rock, to hold things together even when everything felt like it was falling apart. But the more he bottled up his own pain, the more distant he became. He could see the same thing happening with Ethan—his son's anger and frustration simmering just beneath the surface, never fully expressed, always threatening to boil over. Allison, too, had started to withdraw, her once vibrant curiosity dimmed by the uncertainty of their new life.

It wasn't until one evening, when the weight of it all became too much, that Asher realized how wrong he'd been. He had received a particularly difficult letter from Ethan, full of raw emotion, frustration, and confusion. His son's words were heartbreaking: "I don't know who I'm supposed to be anymore, Papa. I don't know if I belong here, or anywhere. It feels like nothing will ever make sense again." As Asher read those words, the dam he'd built around his own feelings began to crack.

For so long, he had been telling Ethan and Allison that everything would be okay. He had promised them that they would figure things out, that they would be fine. But in truth, Asher didn't know if they would. He was just as scared, just as uncertain, as they were. And for the first time, sitting alone in his room with Ethan's letter in his hands, Asher allowed himself to feel the full weight of that fear. The loneliness. The exhaustion. The overwhelming responsibility of trying to rebuild their lives on his own.

And in that moment, Asher made a decision. He wouldn't hide behind his strength anymore. He wouldn't pretend that he had all the answers, because he didn't. What his children needed wasn't a father who had everything figured out—they needed a father who was willing to be real with them, who was willing to admit that he, too, was struggling.

That night, Asher sat down and wrote a letter to Ethan. It was one of the hardest things he had ever written, not because of the words themselves, but because of the honesty they required.

"Ethan," he wrote, his hand trembling slightly, "I've been telling you that everything is going to be okay, but the truth is, I don't know. I don't have all the answers, and I'm scared too. I miss home, just like you do. I miss the life we had before all of this. But we're in this together. You, me, and Allison. And even though things feel impossible right now, we'll figure it out. Not because we have to be strong all the time, but because we're allowed to feel everything that comes with this—anger, sadness, confusion, all of it. It's okay to feel lost sometimes. I do too."

When Asher sealed the letter and slipped it into Ethan's room, he felt a strange sense of relief. It was the first time in months that he had been honest—not just with his children, but with himself. He didn't have to be perfect. He didn't have to be invincible. And maybe, just maybe, that was okay.

Ethan's response came a few days later. His usual anger had softened into something quieter, more introspective. In his letter, Ethan confessed how much he had been struggling to fit in at school, how he felt like an outsider in a place where everyone else seemed to know who they were. But there was a shift in his tone—less defensive, more open.

"I didn't know you felt like this too," Ethan wrote. "I thought I was the only one who was lost. It helps to know that you're feeling it too, that I'm not the only one who doesn't have it all together."

For Ethan, this was the first time he had seen his father as something more than just Papa—the one who always had the answers, the one who never seemed to waver. Seeing Asher's vulnerability allowed Ethan to feel like he could be vulnerable too, and that changed everything. It opened a door for conversations they had both been avoiding, conversations about the pain of the divorce, about the fear of starting over in a new country, about the uncertainty of the future.

Allison, too, began to open up. She had been the quietest of the three, her letters filled with small observations but never delving too deeply into her feelings. But one afternoon, after receiving a letter from Ethan where he shared how difficult it had been for him to make friends, Allison decided to write back with her own truth.

"I miss home too," she wrote. "I miss Mama, and I miss our house. Sometimes I feel like if I close my eyes, I can still smell her cooking, and it makes me sad that we're not there anymore. But I'm also scared that if I don't think about it, I'll forget what home used to feel like. I don't know if that makes sense."

It made perfect sense to Ethan and Asher. They had both been holding on to pieces of the past, afraid that letting go would mean losing it forever. But through their letters, they began to see that letting go wasn't about forgetting—it was about making room for something new.

As the weeks passed, something remarkable began to happen. The family's willingness to be vulnerable with one another created a safe space for healing. They no longer had to pretend to be fine all the time. They could share their fears, their insecurities, and their hopes without judgment. Asher started having more open conversations with Ethan and Allison, not just about their day-to-day lives, but about how they were really feeling. It wasn't always easy—there were still moments of frustration, of anger—but there was also a deeper understanding growing between them.

Ethan, in particular, began to find solace in these moments of honesty. He started journaling more, using the pages to explore his thoughts and emotions. In one entry, he wrote about how difficult it had been to feel like he didn't belong at school, but he also wrote about the small victories—like the time he made a classmate laugh with a joke, or when his soccer coach complimented his improvement on the field.

"I guess it's not always going to be bad," Ethan wrote. "Maybe I can make this work. Maybe I can figure out who I'm supposed to be here."

For Allison, the transformation was quieter but no less profound. She continued to explore her identity through her letters and drawings, using art as a way to express the things she couldn't always put into words. Her letters became more reflective, filled with questions about who she was and where she belonged, but also with a growing sense of curiosity about the new life they were building.

"I'm still not sure where I fit," Allison wrote to her father one evening, "but I think that's okay. Maybe I don't have to know yet. Maybe I'm still figuring it out, and that's what makes this part of life special."

As they embraced vulnerability in their relationships with each other, Asher, Ethan, and Allison found the courage to extend this openness to their new community. Asher, who had once been hesitant to ask for help, began reaching out more—to neighbors, to colleagues, even to the support group he had reluctantly joined. He shared his story with other single parents, learning from their experiences and offering his own insights in return. It wasn't just about finding solutions to his problems; it was about creating a network of people who understood, people who could relate.

Ethan, too, began to open up at school. He started talking more with his classmates, sharing bits of his life back in California, his love for soccer, and his passion for video games. Slowly, he began to form connections, friendships that gave him a sense of belonging he had feared he would never find. It wasn't perfect, but it was a start.

Allison found her own way of connecting through her artwork. She shared her drawings with her classmates, who were fascinated by the way she blended American and Filipino styles in her sketches. Her art became a bridge between the two cultures she was learning to navigate, and through it, she found new friends who appreciated her creativity and saw her for who she truly was.

In the end, vulnerability didn't just heal their family—it strengthened it. Asher, Ethan, and Allison discovered that opening their hearts to each other, and to the world around them, wasn't a sign of fragility. It was an act of courage. It allowed them to form deeper, more meaningful connections, to create a life that was built not on pretending everything was fine, but on the honesty that sometimes, things weren't. And that was okay.

Their journey became a testament to the power of vulnerability—the power to transform pain into growth, fear into resilience, and uncertainty into hope. They learned that being open, being real, was the key to finding their way through the darkness and into a future where they could rebuild, together.

REDISCOVERING FAMILY TRADITIONS

In the whirlwind of their new life in the Philippines, Asher, Ethan, and Allison found themselves feeling adrift, missing the comforts of their old life in California. Their transition had been filled with confusion, excitement, and the endless complexities of starting over. But despite all the newness surrounding them, something was missing—those intangible threads that had always held them together. The traditions. The familiar smells, sounds, and celebrations that had once anchored their lives and made them feel like a family, no matter what was happening in the world outside.

As the weeks turned into months, they realized that no matter how far they had traveled, they could still carry a piece of home with them. It wasn't about geography. It was about the rituals and traditions that had always made them feel connected. And slowly, through their letters and emails, they began to reach back into the past, weaving those cherished memories into their new reality.

It started with Ethan.

One afternoon, Ethan found himself staring at the pantry, searching for something—anything—that would remind him of his grandmother's kitchen. Back in California, she had always cooked the most incredible meals, filling their home with the rich, comforting smells of Filipino dishes that made him feel safe. Now, halfway across the world, Ethan missed those meals more than he cared to admit. He missed the sound of his grandmother bustling around the kitchen, the sizzle of garlic hitting hot oil, the warmth of family gathered around the table, laughing and sharing stories.

In that moment, Ethan decided he would try to recreate his grandmother's famous adobo. He wasn't much of a cook, but he remembered watching her, the way she'd move with such confidence, a pinch of this, a dash of that, never measuring, always trusting her instincts. It was more than just food—it was a tradition, one that he wanted to carry on, even here, in this foreign place.

He sent an email to his father that evening, detailing his ambitious plan. "Papa," he wrote, his tone a mix of determination and uncertainty, "I'm going to try and make Lola's adobo. I found some of the ingredients at the market today. It might not turn out as good as hers, but I think I can do it. The apartment might smell like garlic for days, though. I'll let you know how it goes."

Asher smiled when he read the email. Ethan's desire to recreate that simple, beloved family dish was more than just an attempt to satisfy a craving—it was an act of connection, a way to hold onto something familiar in the midst of so much change. Asher knew what it felt like to miss home, to miss the people and the comforts that made you feel like yourself. He was proud of his son for trying to bring a little bit of that back into their lives.

The next morning, Ethan tackled the recipe with a fierce determination, chopping garlic and onions with more confidence than he felt, marinating the chicken, and slowly simmering the dish until the apartment was filled with the intoxicating aroma of soy sauce, vinegar, and peppercorns. As he stirred the pot, memories flooded back—his grandmother's laugh, the way she would hum softly to herself as she cooked, the stories she told about growing up in the Philippines.

The meal didn't turn out exactly like his grandmother's. It was a little too salty, the chicken a bit overcooked, but none of that mattered. When Ethan sat down to eat, he felt something he hadn't felt since they'd moved—a sense of home, of belonging. He sent another email to his father that evening, proudly reporting that the adobo had been a success. "It wasn't perfect," he admitted, "but it tasted like home. I think Lola would have been proud."

While Ethan was busy reconnecting with their family's culinary traditions, Allison was rediscovering her own love for the festivals they used to celebrate back home. She remembered how, every year, their neighborhood in California would come alive with decorations and celebrations during holidays like Christmas and Easter. But what she missed the most were the lanterns—those beautiful paper creations that her mother used to help her make, their colorful light filling their house with warmth and joy during the holidays.

Now, in this new place, with new friends, Allison wanted to share that part of her culture. She had learned that the school would be hosting a festival soon, one that brought together students from all backgrounds to celebrate their unique traditions. It was the perfect opportunity to introduce her classmates to something that had always made her feel connected to home.

In her journal, Allison excitedly detailed her plans. "I'm going to teach my friends how to make paper lanterns for the festival! Mama used to make them with me, and I think it's the perfect way to bring a little bit of our old life into this new one. I can't wait to see how they turn out."

Allison spent the next week gathering supplies, her small hands carefully folding and cutting the paper, just like her mother had shown her. She taught her friends how to create intricate designs, showing them how to make each fold just right so that the lanterns would hold their shape. It wasn't long before the classroom was filled with a rainbow of lanterns, each one a testament to the beauty of blending old traditions with new friendships.

On the day of the festival, as the lanterns hung from the ceiling, casting a soft glow over the room, Allison felt a surge of pride. Her classmates marveled at the delicate beauty of the lanterns, asking her questions about how she'd learned to make them, what they symbolized. For the first time since moving, Allison didn't feel like the "new girl" anymore. She felt like a part of something, like she had shared a piece of her heart with the people around her.

That night, she wrote in her journal, "Today felt like home. It wasn't the same as our old life, but it was close. I think Mama would have loved it."

As Asher watched his children embrace these traditions—Ethan in the kitchen, Allison at her school festival—he felt a swell of pride. They were finding their way, piece by piece, not by letting go of the past but by bringing it with them into the future. These small acts of cultural preservation—cooking familiar dishes, making lanterns—became powerful symbols of their resilience and adaptability. They were finding ways to blend their old life with their new one, creating something beautiful out of the challenges they faced.

Asher decided it was time to contribute in his own way. He sat down one evening and wrote a letter to Ethan and Allison, reflecting on everything they had been through.

"I'm so proud of you both," he began. "I know this move has been hard, and I know we all miss home. But I see how you're both finding ways to keep our traditions alive, even in the middle of all this change. Ethan, your grandmother would have been so proud of your adobo. Allison, I know your mother is smiling down on you every time you make those lanterns. You're both holding on to the best parts of where we came from, and you're doing it in a way that lets us move forward."

Asher paused, thinking about what it meant to balance the old with the new. He had always believed that keeping traditions alive was important, but now he understood that it wasn't just about maintaining a link to the past—it was about building something new, something that blended their heritage with the possibilities of their new life in the Philippines.

"We don't have to leave our past behind," he wrote, "but we also don't have to be stuck in it. We can take the best parts with us, carry them forward, and let them evolve as we grow. That's what traditions are—they're living things, meant to change with us. And that's how we'll make this new place feel like home."

The letter was more than just words—it was a reminder that their journey wasn't about leaving behind who they were, but about discovering how to be themselves in a new context. Asher knew that as long as they held onto the things that mattered—family, tradition, and love—they could make any place their home.

As the months went by, the family continued to blend their old traditions with their new life. Ethan experimented with more Filipino dishes, learning from local cooks and even sharing recipes with his friends. Allison became known at school for her creativity, always coming up with new ways to incorporate her cultural heritage into the projects they worked on. And Asher, inspired by his children's resilience, began to embrace the new customs and celebrations of their adopted country, finding joy in the ways they mirrored—and sometimes enhanced—the traditions he had grown up with.

The power of these traditions wasn't just in the comfort they brought—it was in the way they allowed the family to grow and adapt. Each recipe cooked, each lantern made, each memory shared was a step toward healing, a way to bridge the gap between the life they had left behind and the one they were building.

By rediscovering and reimagining their family traditions, Asher, Ethan, and Allison found a renewed sense of identity and belonging in their adopted country. They realized that home wasn't just a place—it was something they carried with them, something they created together, no matter where they were.

Their journey of healing and adaptation became a testament to the strength of family traditions, not as relics of the past, but as living threads that connected them to both their history and their future. Through these rituals, they found a way to stay grounded in who they were, even as they embraced the possibilities of who they could become.

CHAPTER 6
PART V: GROWING PAINS

∙∙∙∙∙∙∙∙∙∙∙∙∙∙∙∙∙∙∙∙∙∙∙∙∙∙∙∙∙

Asher's Career Struggles and Triumphs

In the wake of our family's upheaval, I found myself not only navigating the emotional storm of divorce but also confronting the daunting challenge of rebuilding my career in a country that felt, at times, completely foreign. My professional life, once a steady pillar I could rely on, suddenly felt fragile. The weight of providing for Ethan and Allison pressed on me more heavily with each passing day, and the letters I wrote to them during this time were laced with both determination and vulnerability.

Every morning, I'd sit at the kitchen table, laptop open, searching job boards and sending out applications. The screen felt cold and distant, like a wall between my old life and the future I was trying to carve out. The Philippine job market was competitive, unfamiliar, and I often wondered if my skills from California would even translate here. It was as though I was starting from scratch—an experience both humbling and terrifying.

The first few weeks were rough. My inbox filled with automated rejection emails, polite but impersonal, thanking me for my interest but regretting to inform me that I hadn't been selected. Those letters piled up like a mountain of doubt. I could feel the pressure

Letters From The Heart

building inside me, wondering how long I could sustain this new life if nothing panned out.

In my letters to Ethan and Allison, I tried to hide the worst of my frustration, but I couldn't mask it completely. I wrote about the endless interviews that seemed to go nowhere, the polite rejections that stung more each time, and the sleepless nights spent worrying about what would come next.

"Hey kids," I'd write, "today wasn't easy. Another interview didn't go as planned, but I'm going to keep trying. I know this will turn around. We just need to be patient, and I promise I'll figure this out."

But even as I shared my struggles with them, I found myself drawing strength from the resilience I saw in them. Every day, Ethan and Allison faced their own challenges—making friends at their new school, adapting to the language, finding their place in this unfamiliar country. They didn't give up. They showed up every day, determined to make it work. And if they could do that, then I owed it to them to do the same.

I remember one night in particular, after receiving yet another rejection, I sat down at my desk, exhausted and dejected. I was about to write a letter to the kids, but the words wouldn't come. All I could think about was the pressure of being their provider, their constant, the one who was supposed to keep things together. And yet, I felt like I was failing. But as I sat there, my mind wandered back to something Allison had written in one of her journal entries. She had described how, even though school was hard and she missed home, she was trying to learn Tagalog one word at a time. "It's hard, Papa," she'd written, "but I'm not giving up."

Her words stuck with me. If my daughter could face her own struggles head-on, then so could I.

The next morning, I tackled my job search with a renewed sense of purpose. I refined my approach, researched companies more thoroughly, and networked harder than ever. Each application became less about desperation and more about persistence. Slowly, the tide began to turn.

Opportunities started to appear—not the big, dream jobs I had once hoped for, but small steps in the right direction. I was invited to a second interview for a mid-level position at a marketing agency. Then, I received a call from a tech company interested in my background in project management. These small victories felt monumental in the context of everything we had been through, and I made sure to share them with Ethan and Allison. Our correspondence began to take on a different tone—not just about my struggles, but about our collective perseverance.

"Ethan, Allison," I wrote one day, "I wanted to tell you some good news. I had a really great interview today, and it looks like things are starting to pick up. It's not easy, but we're making progress. Just like you guys are finding your way at school, I'm finding my way at work. I'm so proud of both of you, and I hope you know that we're in this together. We'll keep moving forward."

In those moments, I realized that my struggles weren't just mine to carry. We were all in this new chapter of life together, and sharing both the highs and lows with Ethan and Allison helped us all feel more connected. It was no longer just about me trying to provide for them—it was about us supporting one another in this unfamiliar territory.

Then, one day, the breakthrough came.

I received an offer from a local tech company, not for an entry-level position, but as a project manager—exactly the kind of role that aligned with my skills and experience. It wasn't just a job—it was a validation, a reminder that I hadn't lost my footing entirely, that I still had something valuable to contribute. When I received the offer letter, I sat at my desk for a long time, just staring at it, trying to take it all in. Relief washed over me like a wave. We had made it through the worst of the storm.

That evening, I wrote a letter to Ethan and Allison, my heart full of gratitude and hope.

"Hey Kiddos, I did it. I got the job. It's not just any job, but one that I know I can do well—one that will help us build the future we've been working toward. I can't tell you how proud I am of both of you for being patient with me and for supporting me even when things were tough. This is just the beginning. Things are going to get better from here."

When I finally started that job, it came with its own set of challenges—adapting to a new work culture, learning the ropes in a country where business practices were different from what I'd been used to. But there was also immense satisfaction. I found myself energized by the work, by the chance to contribute and grow professionally again. It wasn't just about earning a paycheck—it was about rebuilding my sense of self, proving to myself and my children that we could find success and stability here.

I shared these new experiences with Ethan and Allison, too, in the form of stories about my day-to-day life at work. I told them about the projects I was managing, the colleagues I was meeting, and the small victories I celebrated along the way. One day, I wrote to them about the joy of completing a big project, one that had felt insurmountable at the start but had turned into a great success.

"It's funny," I wrote, "how much this job reminds me of what we've been going through as a family. At first, it felt impossible—like I wouldn't be able to do it. But step by step, I figured it out. I found my rhythm. And now, things are looking up. Just like they are for all of us."

As the weeks passed, our family grew stronger, not just because I had found stability in my career, but because we had learned to rely on each other. Ethan and Allison had become my inspiration during the hardest days, and now, as we began to settle into our new life, I could see how our shared journey had made us closer.

In our letters, we no longer talked just about the struggles—we talked about the future. About what we wanted to do next, about the dreams we had for this new chapter of our lives. For Ethan, it was about joining the school soccer team and making more friends. For Allison, it was about exploring her artistic side, maybe even taking an art class. And for me, it was about continuing to grow in my new job, learning more about the tech industry, and maybe even pursuing a leadership role someday.

We had all faced challenges we never expected, but through it all, we had discovered something even more important: resilience. The ability to keep moving forward, even when everything felt impossible.

The bond between the three of us had deepened in ways I hadn't imagined. We had learned that it was okay to struggle, okay to be vulnerable, okay to ask for help. And now, standing on the other side of that difficult chapter, I knew that whatever came next, we would face it together.

In one of my last letters before we transitioned to regular conversations about our daily lives, I wrote to Ethan and Allison about the most important lesson I had learned through all of this.

"Kids, no matter what happens, remember this: we're a team. We've been through so much already, and we're still standing. That's not because we're perfect or because we have all the answers—it's because we don't give up. We keep going, no matter what. And that's what makes us strong."

Through the ups and downs, the struggles and triumphs, we had rediscovered not only our strength as individuals but our strength as a family. And that, more than any job or any victory, was the greatest success of all.

ETHAN'S COMING OF AGE

Dear Papa,

As I sit here, thinking about how far we've come, I realize that I'm not the same person I was when we first arrived here. I'm writing this letter because I want to tell you about the things I've been thinking—about who I was, who I am now, and where I'm headed. I guess you could say this is the letter of a boy who's no longer a boy anymore.

    I didn't know it then, but everything changed for me the day we left California. I was angry, confused, and lost. I blamed you, I blamed Mama, and I blamed the world. It felt like everything I knew had been ripped away. You know how hard it was for me—I didn't hide it. The divorce hit me like a tidal wave, and when we moved to the Philippines, it felt like I was being dragged out to sea with no way to swim back to shore. I couldn't understand why our family had to fall apart, and I carried that anger with me for a long time. I pushed you away, and I'm sorry for that.

    But as I look back now, I can see that all of those struggles shaped me into the person I'm becoming. It wasn't easy, but maybe it wasn't supposed to be. We've been through so much, but I've realized that life is about facing the hard things, not running from them.

    I want to tell you about some of the things that changed me along the way.

    School was the first real challenge. I remember walking into those halls, hearing kids speak a language I barely understood, seeing them laugh and talk like they had known each other their whole lives. And there I was, the outsider. I didn't know how to fit in. Every day, I thought about what it would be like to go back home. But then something changed.

    It wasn't a big moment. There wasn't a dramatic turning point where everything suddenly made sense. It was more like little pieces falling into place. Like the day Paula sat next to me at lunch. I was sitting alone, like usual, just picking at my food, not wanting to draw attention to myself. She plopped down next to me and started talking, like it was the most natural thing in the world. She didn't care that I was the "new kid" or that I didn't know the right words in Tagalog. She just talked to me. That was the start of everything. Paula became my first real friend here, and through her, I started to feel like I belonged.

She introduced me to her group of friends, and slowly, I began to find my place. They didn't just accept me—they helped me understand that I didn't have to change who I was to fit in. For the first time in a long time, I didn't feel like I had to hide my American side to be accepted. I started embracing it, talking about California, sharing stories of our life back home. And they listened. They made me feel like it was okay to be different.

But fitting in wasn't the only thing that shaped me. You've always told me that life is about learning to balance things, and now I understand what you meant. Living here has made me think a lot about my identity. At first, I felt torn between two worlds—American and Filipino. I didn't know how to merge the two. But then, over time, I realized I didn't have to choose. I could be both.

One night, Paula and I were sitting on the rooftop of her apartment building, looking out at the city lights. We were talking about everything—school, life, the future. I told her about how sometimes I felt like I didn't know where I belonged. And you know what she said? She said, "Ethan, you don't have to belong to just one place. You belong to yourself. That's enough." Her words stuck with me. That night, I stopped worrying so much about trying to fit into a box. I started seeing myself as a person who could hold two identities at once—and be proud of both.

I've also had a lot of mentors along the way. People who have guided me without even knowing it. My soccer coach, for one. He saw potential in me when I didn't see it in myself. I remember one game, I was frustrated because I missed an easy goal, and I felt like I had let the team down. After the game, Coach pulled me aside. He didn't lecture me or make me feel worse. Instead, he said, "Ethan, the only way you get better is by making mistakes. You're allowed to mess up. That's how you grow." I've held on to those words ever since.

It's funny, isn't it? You hear things like that all the time—stuff about how failure helps you grow—but it doesn't really sink in until you experience it for yourself. I've made my share of mistakes, both on and off the field, but I'm learning to forgive myself. I'm learning to see the value in getting it wrong sometimes.

But through it all, the most important thing I've learned is about us—about you and me. I used to be so angry, Papa. I blamed you for everything. I didn't see how hard it was for you, trying to keep everything together for me and Allison. I couldn't see past my own hurt. But now, I get it. I see the sacrifices you made, the way you put us first even when it felt like the world was crumbling around you. You were always there, even when I pushed you away.

I remember the nights you stayed up late, writing letters to me, encouraging me, telling me it would be okay. I didn't want to believe you then, but now I realize how much those words meant. You never gave up on me, even when I gave up on myself. You were the one constant when everything else felt uncertain.

And now, as I'm getting older, I see you differently. You're not just my dad—you're someone I look up to. You've shown me what it means to be strong, not because you never struggle, but because you keep going, even when things get tough. That's the kind of man I want to be.

As for the future? Well, that's something I think about a lot now. I don't have all the answers, and I don't know exactly where I'm headed, but I do know this: I'm ready. I'm ready to face whatever comes next. This journey hasn't been easy, but it's made me stronger. It's helped me understand who I am and who I want to become.

I'm excited for what's ahead. I'm thinking about applying to college, maybe studying something that lets me combine my love for sports and helping people. Paula's been encouraging me to look into sports medicine or physical therapy. I like the idea of doing something that helps others, just like so many people have helped me.

But no matter where I end up, I want you to know that I'm going to make you proud. Everything I've learned from you, from this move, from all the challenges we've faced—it's all helped me grow into the person I am now. And I'm still growing. I'm still learning. But I'm not scared anymore. I'm ready to take on the world, one step at a time.

I guess what I'm really trying to say is thank you. Thank you for being there for me, even when I didn't deserve it. Thank you for pushing me to be better, for believing in me, for showing me that it's okay to struggle, as long as you don't give up. I hope you know how much that means to me.

I know I haven't always made things easy, but I want you to know that I see you. I see everything you've done for me and Allison, and I'm so grateful. I'm proud to be your son.

So, here's to the future—whatever it holds. I'm ready for it, and I know we'll face it together, like we always have.

With all my love,
Ethan

Ethan's journey from a confused, angry boy to a young man on the cusp of adulthood was not defined by any one moment, but by a series of experiences that pushed him to grow, adapt, and embrace the complexity of life. His letter to his father was more than just a reflection—it was a testament to the resilience of the human spirit, to the power of family, and to the lessons we learn when we're willing to face our struggles head-on.

Through Ethan's words, readers witness the transformation of a boy who once felt lost and broken into someone who understands the importance of perseverance, identity, and love. His story is a reminder that even in the midst of life's greatest challenges, there is always room for growth, for healing, and for hope.

ALLISON'S BLOSSOMING TALENTS

Dear Papa,

I wanted to tell you something super exciting! I've been painting! Not just little doodles like before, but real paintings with bright colors, just like the ones we saw in that art gallery back home. I've been using all the colors I can find—blue like the sky back in California, and green like the trees here in the Philippines. It's kind of like I'm painting our old home and our new one all at the same time. Isn't that cool?

I made a picture of our house in California yesterday. Remember the big tree outside? I painted it with those tiny flowers I used to pick for you and Mama. I miss that tree a lot, but now I can see it every day in my painting. I even painted our old front door in red because I liked how it looked when the sun hit it just right. I think it's my best one so far! I wish you could hang it in your office like you used to with my drawings.

Do you know what else I painted? Our new street here! It's so different, Papa. The houses are closer together, and there are so many people walking around all the time. It's kind of loud, but I painted the tricycles and the street vendors just the way I see them. I even added a little stall with fruits, like the ones we see when we go shopping. I think it's fun to paint what's around us now, even though I miss our old neighborhood sometimes.

I think painting helps me feel like I'm telling stories without using words. You know how sometimes I can't find the right words to explain how I feel? Well, when I paint, I don't have to use words. I just let the colors do the talking. When I miss Mama, I paint with warm colors like orange and yellow. When I'm thinking about you and how strong you are, I use deep blues and purples, because they make me feel safe, like you always do.

You know how much I love the sunsets here, right? I painted one last week with all the pink and orange and purple mixed together. The sky here is so big and beautiful, and sometimes it makes me feel like everything is going to be okay. I painted it for you because I wanted you to see it, even if you're busy at work. Maybe it can help you feel happy, like it does for me.

And guess what? I made a new friend in school who loves painting too! Her name is Liza, and she's been teaching me some new tricks with brushes and how to mix colors. We've been painting after school together, and I even showed her how to paint those paper lanterns you taught me to make. It's really fun because now I have someone to paint with, and she loves hearing about our life back in California. We're going to paint a big picture of both our homes—hers here and mine back in the States—and put them together like one big world. Isn't that awesome?

But you know what my favorite painting is, Papa? It's the one I made of us—our family. I painted it yesterday while Ethan was playing video games. I wanted to make sure I got everyone just right. You're standing tall, like always, and I made your eyes look kind, just like when you tell me everything's going to be alright. Ethan's next to you, holding a soccer ball, and I made him smile, even though he doesn't smile as much as he used to. But I know he's happy deep down. And I painted Mama too. She's sitting next to me, and we're all together, like we used to be. It felt nice to paint her again.

I used big, bold colors for all of us because I wanted it to look strong, like our family. Even though things are different now, I know we're still strong together. I hope you like it, Papa. I think it's one of my best.

When I paint, I feel like I'm making a new home. I miss California, but I'm starting to like it here too. There are so many new things to see and paint. I think I'm going to paint our whole journey—maybe one day I'll show people how it felt to move so far away and find a new place to belong. It's hard sometimes, but it's also exciting, don't you think?

Ethan says my paintings make him happy too. He told me the one I did of the family makes him feel like everything is going to be okay. That made me feel really proud. I love painting because it's like I can take all the feelings I have inside and put them on the canvas. Sometimes I'm sad, sometimes I'm happy, but when I paint, it all comes out in a way that makes me feel better.

I'm going to keep painting, Papa, because it makes me feel closer to you and to Mama and to everything that's important to me. I hope when you look at my paintings, you feel happy too.

Love,
Allison

Asher's heart swelled with pride as he read Allison's letter. Her words, brimming with excitement and sincerity, spoke volumes about how deeply she was processing the world around her. She was only seven, but her art was helping her navigate the complexities of their move, the family's past, and the future they were building together.

Allison's paintings weren't just a hobby—they were her way of making sense of the emotions that were often too big for her to express in words. Asher marveled at her ability to take the scattered pieces of their old life and merge them with the new, blending colors and shapes in a way that connected their past, present, and future. Through her art, she was telling a story—a story of loss, change, hope, and, most importantly, resilience.

Ethan had written to Asher about Allison's latest masterpiece, the family portrait. He described it in vivid detail: the bold strokes that represented each family member, the way Allison had painted herself with Mama, even though she was no longer physically there. It was a testament to the deep connection Allison still felt with her mother, and Asher was moved to see how his daughter had used art as a way to keep that bond alive.

"This portrait she painted," Ethan wrote, "it's more than just a picture. It's like she's telling us that no matter how far apart we are, we're still together. It made me feel things, Papa. Like, maybe we'll all be okay after all."

CHAPTER 7
PART VI: HEALING HEARTS

Confronting Emotional Wounds

The quiet moments always had a way of sneaking up on Asher, in between the noise of daily life, the letters, the school drop-offs, the job stress. It was in those moments—the stillness—that the weight of everything he'd been carrying hit him hardest. The pain of the divorce, the guilt that gnawed at him for uprooting Ethan and Allison, and the fear that he was failing them as a single parent in a foreign country. These weren't new feelings; they'd been with him from the start, buried deep beneath the surface. But now, they were demanding to be heard.

One evening, after the kids had gone to bed, Asher sat alone at the kitchen table, a blank page in front of him. His pen hovered over the paper, hesitant, as if releasing the words would make the pain all too real. He had written countless letters to Ethan and Allison over the past months, always filled with encouragement and hope, always striving to be the strong father they needed him to be. But this time was different. This letter was going to be raw, honest. He wasn't going to hide from the truth anymore.

Asher took a deep breath and began to write.

"Dear Ethan and Allison,

I've been thinking a lot lately about everything we've been through—everything I've put you through. And I know that I've tried to stay strong for you both, but I haven't always been honest. There are things I haven't told you, feelings I've buried because I didn't want you to see me struggle. But I think it's time I tell you the truth.

I'm scared.

I'm scared that I made the wrong choice. That moving here, starting over, wasn't the best thing for you. I'm scared that I'm not doing enough, not being the father you deserve. I've been carrying this guilt with me every day, trying to ignore it, but it's time I face it.

The truth is, the divorce hurt me more than I've let on. It hurt to see our family fall apart, and I know it hurt both of you too. But what I want you to know—what I need you to understand—is that none of this was your fault. None of it. I know you've been struggling, and I know I haven't always been there for you the way I should have been. But I'm here now. I'm listening. And I want to hear everything you've been feeling."

As the words flowed onto the page, Asher felt a release, as if the weight of years of emotional baggage had begun to lift. It wasn't an easy letter to write, but he knew it was necessary. Healing wasn't just about pretending everything was okay and moving forward. It was about facing the past, acknowledging the pain, and working through it together. He sealed the letter and placed it in an envelope for Ethan to find in the morning.

Ethan had been wrestling with his own emotional wounds, though he hadn't shared them with anyone, not even his father. His journal had become his refuge, a place where he could release the anger and confusion that had been bubbling inside of him since the divorce. His entries were raw, filled with questions he didn't know how to answer.

"Why did everything have to change?

Why did Mama leave?

Why do I feel so lost here?"

The pages of his journal were stained with his frustration, his sense of abandonment. He was angry at his mother for leaving, angry at his father for dragging them halfway across the world, and angry at himself for not knowing how to cope. Every day, Ethan struggled to fit in at his new school, to make sense of the new life they were building. He missed California, missed the friends he'd left behind, missed the sense of normalcy that had been stripped away from him.

But as time passed, Ethan's entries began to shift. He started writing about Paula, his first real friend in the Philippines, who had been his anchor in the storm of change. He wrote about soccer and how it had become his escape, a place where he could just be himself, free from the expectations and pressures of everything else. Slowly, the anger began to give way to something else—something softer, more reflective.

"I think I'm starting to understand things better now. It still hurts, but maybe it's okay to hurt. Maybe it's part of getting stronger."

Allison's journey was quieter, but no less profound. As the youngest, her emotions often came in bursts—moments of sadness, flashes of frustration, followed by stretches of silence where she retreated into her drawings. Her journal entries were short, often just a few lines, but they carried the weight of her innocence grappling with the confusion of adult decisions.

"I miss Mama.

I miss our old house.

Why can't we all be together again?"

Allison's art became her outlet, her way of processing emotions too big for words. She painted their old life in California—the house, the tree in the front yard, her mother's face. And then, she painted their new life in the Philippines—the bustling streets, the colorful markets, the tricycles zipping by. It was her way of bridging the gap between the life they'd lost and the one they were trying to build.

One evening, after reading one of her father's letters, Allison picked up her paintbrush and began working on her most ambitious painting yet. It was a family portrait, but this time, she painted them all together—her, Ethan, Papa, and Mama. It wasn't a literal representation; it was a blend of memories and hopes. She painted them standing under the big tree from their old home, but in the background, she added the colors of the Philippine sunset. It was a picture of their family as she wished it could be, all together, despite the distance and the changes.

As the weeks passed, the family's letters, journal entries, and conversations became more open, more honest. They were learning to name their emotions, to share their vulnerabilities with one another. Asher was no longer afraid to admit his fears to Ethan and Allison, and in turn, they began to open up about their own struggles.

One night, the three of them sat together in the living room, surrounded by letters and journals. It had been months since they had all truly talked about what they had been through, and the silence felt heavy at first. But then, Ethan broke the quiet.

"Papa, I read your letter. I know you feel guilty about everything that happened, but I don't want you to. I was angry for a long time, and I blamed you and Mama. But I don't anymore. I get it now. We're all just trying to figure this out."

Asher felt a lump in his throat. Ethan's words were more mature than his years, and for the first time, Asher realized that his son was no longer a boy—he was growing into a young man.

"I've been scared too," Allison added, her voice small but steady. "I didn't know how to tell you because I didn't want to make you sad. But I miss Mama, and I miss how things used to be. But I'm happy here too. I just didn't know how to say it."

Asher reached for Allison's hand and squeezed it gently. "It's okay to feel both, Allison. It's okay to miss the past and still be excited about the future. We can hold onto the memories while we make new ones."

The conversation flowed easily after that, as if a dam had been broken. They talked about everything—the divorce, the move, their fears and hopes. They laughed, they cried, and they shared stories from the past few months, each one a testament to the strength they had found in one another.

In the days that followed, something shifted. The weight of the past was still there, but it didn't feel as heavy anymore. They were no longer running from their pain—they were facing it, together. Asher could see the changes in his children. Ethan walked with more confidence, his anger slowly melting away as he found his place in their new world. Allison smiled more, her paintings reflecting a mix of old memories and new experiences. And Asher himself felt lighter, more at peace with the choices he had made.

Healing, they had learned, wasn't about pretending the wounds weren't there. It was about confronting them, facing the pain head-on, and allowing themselves to feel it. It was about sharing that pain with the people they loved and finding strength in vulnerability.

Through their letters, journal entries, and late-night conversations, Asher, Ethan, and Allison had begun to rebuild not just their lives, but their family. They were creating something new, something stronger. And as they looked ahead to the future, they knew that no matter what challenges came their way, they would face them together.

In confronting their emotional wounds, they had discovered the true meaning of resilience—not the absence of pain, but the courage to move through it. And in that courage, they had found healing.

THE ART OF FORGIVENESS

Forgiveness is a word Asher had always understood, but it wasn't until the quiet nights in Manila that he truly began to grasp its depth. It wasn't just about saying the words or offering an apology; forgiveness was about the internal struggle, the journey to release the heavy burdens that weighed down the heart. For Asher, Ethan, and Allison, forgiveness was not a single moment, but a continuous process—a daily decision to let go of the pain and move forward together.

The hardest part of forgiveness wasn't about forgiving others. It was about forgiving himself.

Asher had carried guilt since the divorce, guilt for the ways things had unraveled and the decisions that had led them here. He blamed himself for the upheaval in his children's lives, for uprooting them from California to a place so foreign. The move to the Philippines was supposed to be a fresh start, a chance to rebuild, but it also felt like an escape—from his past, from the pain of a marriage that had fallen apart. And yet, here he was, unable to escape the one thing that still haunted him: the guilt.

As Asher sat down to write a letter to Ethan and Allison one evening, he hesitated. How could he teach them about forgiveness if he hadn't fully embraced it himself? How could he ask them to forgive their mother, to forgive him, if he still clung to the mistakes he had made?

He began writing slowly, the pen heavy in his hand.
"Dear Ethan and Allison,

I've been thinking a lot about forgiveness lately. It's something we talk about, something we know we're supposed to do, but it's also one of the hardest things to actually practice. I've realized that I've been holding onto things that I need to let go of—not just the hurt from the divorce, but my own mistakes. I haven't been able to forgive myself for some of the choices I made, and I think it's time that I do."

Asher paused, feeling the weight of the words. He had never said it out loud before, never admitted that he had been punishing himself all this time. But as he wrote, he began to understand that forgiveness wasn't just for others—it was for him too. He needed to let go of the resentment, the "what ifs," and the guilt if he was going to move forward and be the father his children needed him to be.

"I want you both to know something important," Asher continued. "Forgiving someone doesn't mean you're saying that what happened was okay. It doesn't mean that the hurt disappears overnight. What it means is that you're choosing not to let that hurt control you anymore. Forgiveness is about freeing yourself from the anger, the resentment, and the pain so you can move forward."

As Asher finished the letter, he felt lighter. It was a small step, but an important one. He couldn't change the past, but he could choose how to move forward. He folded the letter carefully and slipped it into an envelope, leaving it on the kitchen table for Ethan and Allison to read in the morning.

Ethan's journey to forgiveness was different. His anger had been simmering beneath the surface for so long that he wasn't sure he even knew how to let it go. He had been angry at his father for dragging them across the world, angry at his mother for leaving, and angry at himself for not being able to fix it. Forgiveness felt like a mountain too high to climb, a task that required more strength than he thought he had.

But something had shifted in Ethan over the past few months. His letters to his father had become more open, more vulnerable. He had started talking about the things that had hurt him, the things he had been afraid to admit for so long. And in that honesty, Ethan began to see that his anger was only hurting him. Holding onto it wasn't making anything better—it was just keeping him stuck in the past.

One night, after reading Asher's letter about forgiveness, Ethan picked up his own pen. His handwriting was careful, deliberate, as he tried to put into words the emotions he had been carrying for so long.

"Papa,

I think you're right about forgiveness. It's hard. I've been angry for so long, and I didn't know how to let it go. But I'm starting to realize that holding onto that anger isn't helping me anymore. It's just making things harder. I've been mad at you and Mama, but mostly, I've been mad at myself for not being able to fix things. I wanted everything to go back to the way it was, but now I know that's not possible."

Ethan hesitated for a moment, the next sentence feeling heavier than the rest.

"I forgive you, Papa. And I forgive Mama too. I know you both did the best you could. I'm still sad sometimes, but I don't want to be angry anymore. I want to move forward."

For Ethan, those words were a release. The weight he had been carrying began to lift, little by little. Forgiving his parents didn't erase the pain of the divorce or the difficulty of adjusting to their new life, but it allowed him to start healing. It gave him the freedom to stop clinging to the past and start embracing the present.

Allison's path to forgiveness was softer, gentler, but no less important. As the youngest, she had often felt caught in the middle of her parents' separation, too young to fully understand what was happening but old enough to feel the sadness that had settled over their family. Her art had become her refuge, a way to process the emotions that were too big for her to put into words. Through her paintings, Allison expressed the longing she felt for her mother, the confusion of their new life, and the quiet hope that things would one day get better.

One afternoon, as Allison painted in her room, she decided to write a letter to her mother. She hadn't written to her in a while, unsure of what to say. But now, as the colors of the sunset bled across her canvas, she felt ready. Allison's letter was simple, but filled with the innocent wisdom of a child who was learning to forgive.

"Dear Mama,

I miss you. I wish you were here with us. I've been painting a lot, and I think you'd like my pictures. I painted one of you and me together, like we used to be. It makes me feel better when I look at it."

Allison paused, chewing on the end of her pencil, thinking of what to write next. She wasn't angry at her mother, but she had felt a deep sadness since the divorce, a sadness that had been hard to shake. But as she wrote, she realized that she wasn't holding onto that sadness anymore.

"I know you couldn't stay with us, and that's okay. I'm not mad at you. I just miss you. But I'm happy here too. I think it's okay to feel both. I love you, Mama."

Allison signed the letter with a heart, the way she always did, and set it aside to mail. It was her way of letting go of the hurt, of accepting that their family had changed but that love could still remain.

As the days passed, forgiveness became a quiet, powerful presence in their lives. Asher found peace in forgiving his ex-wife—not for her sake, but for his own. He didn't want to carry the bitterness anymore. He wanted to set a positive example for Ethan and Allison, to show them that forgiveness wasn't about forgetting, but about freeing yourself from the weight of resentment.

Ethan, too, found strength in forgiveness. He began to see his parents not as the cause of his pain, but as people who were doing their best in a difficult situation. And in forgiving them, he found the freedom to move forward with his own life, unburdened by the anger that had once held him back.

For Allison, forgiveness was a natural part of her healing process. Her letters to her mother became more frequent, filled with love and hope. Her art blossomed as she embraced the new life they were building, no longer tethered to the sadness of the past.

In the end, the art of forgiveness became the cornerstone of the family's healing. It wasn't easy, and it didn't happen all at once.

But through their letters, their conversations, and their quiet moments of reflection, Asher, Ethan, and Allison learned that forgiveness wasn't about erasing the past. It was about choosing to let go of the pain, to open their hearts to new possibilities, and to embrace the life they were creating together.

The act of forgiveness became a transformative force, allowing them to rediscover joy, rebuild their relationships, and create a future free from the weight of past hurts. It was a reminder that even in the face of life's greatest challenges, forgiveness had the power to heal, to strengthen, and to set them free.

REDEFINING FAMILY

In the months following their divorce and relocation, Asher, Ethan, and Allison found themselves navigating the unfamiliar terrain of what it meant to be a family. The life they had known—filled with predictable routines, familiar faces, and the comfortable stability of a two-parent household—was now a thing of the past. They were in a new country, their once-solid foundation fractured by change. The idea of family, once simple and straightforward, had become something they had to rediscover, redefine, and rebuild from the ground up.

Their letters and journal entries captured this delicate transformation, each word reflecting the evolving dynamics within their small but resilient household. For Asher, there were nights when the weight of responsibility felt almost unbearable. In the quiet moments after the kids had gone to bed, he would sit at the kitchen table, pen in hand, struggling to find the words that could convey both his love and his uncertainty. He knew that he couldn't replace the stability of their old life, but he was determined to create something new—something that would show Ethan and Allison that family was more than just a mother and father under one roof.

In one of his letters to the children, Asher opened up about his doubts and his hopes.

"Dear Ethan and Allison,

I've been thinking a lot about what family means. It used to be simple for us, didn't it? We had our traditions, our routines, our way of doing things. But now that everything has changed, I've realized something. Family isn't just about who's around the dinner table. It's about the love we have for each other, the way we take care of one another, no matter what. It's about finding new ways to be together, to laugh, to support each other, even when things feel different.

I know this move has been hard. I know things aren't the same without your mother here, but that doesn't mean we can't create something beautiful out of what we have now. We're still a family. We always will be. And I promise you, we'll figure this out together."

As Asher wrote, he could feel the tension in his shoulders ease just a bit. He wasn't sure if his words would bring comfort, but he hoped they would help Ethan and Allison see that family wasn't broken, just evolving.

For Ethan, redefining family had been more challenging. He had spent months angry at the changes, feeling like his world had been turned upside down. His journal entries reflected the inner battle he waged between accepting their new reality and clinging to the life they had left behind.

"I miss how things used to be," he had written one night, his words raw with frustration. "I miss having Mama around, and I miss the way things felt... normal. I don't know how to move forward when everything feels so messed up."

But slowly, as weeks turned into months, Ethan began to see that their family wasn't as broken as he had once thought. It wasn't the same, but that didn't mean it was less. Through their letters and conversations, he began to understand that family could take many forms, and the love they shared hadn't disappeared—it had simply shifted, adapting to fit their new circumstances.

Ethan found solace in the unexpected connections they had begun to form within their new community. At first, he had been resistant to meeting new people. He missed his friends back home, and the idea of trying to make new ones felt exhausting. But over time, the sense of loneliness began to fade as he started building friendships with other kids in the neighborhood.

In one letter to his father, Ethan described an evening that had left a lasting impression on him.

"Papa,

Tonight was... different. But in a good way. We had dinner at Mrs. Erin Connelly's house with a bunch of neighbors, and it felt weird at first because I didn't know anyone. But after a while, it was kind of fun. There was so much food, and everyone was laughing and sharing stories. It made me realize something—I think this is what you meant when you said family doesn't have to be just blood. I didn't know these people before, but they made us feel like we belonged. And I guess that's what matters, right?"

For Ethan, that evening was a turning point. It was the first time since their move that he began to see their new life not as a detour, but as a new path with its own possibilities. He had started to let go of the bitterness that had clung to him, making space for the connections and friendships that were blossoming around them.

Allison, with her wide-eyed curiosity and tender heart, had always been the one to accept change more easily. But even she had struggled with the absence of her mother and the unfamiliarity of their new home. Her paintings, filled with vibrant colors and swirling patterns, became a visual representation of the way she was processing the world around her. She painted their old house in California, the tree she used to climb, the sunsets she missed. But alongside these images, she began to paint new ones—the bustling markets of Manila, the neighbors who had become friends, the places where she and Ethan played after school.

In one of her journal entries, Allison wrote about a new tradition she wanted to start, one that blended their past with their present.

"I've been thinking about Christmas. I know it's going to be different this year without Mama, but maybe we can make it special in a new way. What if we make our own lanterns to hang up? I learned how to make them in art class, and I think it would be fun! We can still do the things we used to do, like bake cookies and sing songs, but maybe we can add some new things too. That way, it's like we're making a new kind of Christmas, just for us."

Asher smiled when he read her words. Allison, in her quiet way, was teaching them all that moving forward didn't mean leaving everything behind. It meant carrying the best parts of the past with them, while making room for new traditions that could grow alongside them.

As the months passed, the family's new life began to take shape. It wasn't without its challenges—there were still moments of grief, of longing for the way things had been. But there were also moments of joy, of connection, and of a growing understanding that family wasn't confined to the traditional structure they had once known.

They had formed unexpected bonds with their neighbors, colleagues, and fellow expatriates. There were potluck dinners where everyone brought dishes from their own countries, cultural exchange nights where they learned about different customs, and impromptu playdates with kids from all walks of life. These experiences filled their once-empty evenings with laughter and warmth, reminding them that family could extend far beyond blood.

One night, as they sat together on the couch, Asher looked around at Ethan and Allison, both of them tired but smiling after a long day. The house, once filled with a heavy silence, now hummed with a quiet contentment. It wasn't the life they had planned, but it was a life they were learning to love.

In one of his final letters to his children, Asher summed up what had taken them months to discover.

"Dear Ethan and Allison,

I've been thinking about family again. I used to think that family was something you were born into, something that never changed. But now I see that family is something we create, something that grows and evolves with us. It's about the people who are there for you, the ones who make you feel safe and loved, even when everything else is uncertain.

We've been through a lot, and I know it hasn't been easy. But I want you both to know how proud I am of you—of how strong you've been, and how much you've grown. We may not be the family we once were, but we are still a family. And that's something I wouldn't trade for anything."

Ethan and Allison's responses reflected the same quiet understanding. They had come to realize that family wasn't defined by the number of people in the household, or by sticking to the old ways of doing things. It was defined by the love and support they gave each other, by the way they continued to show up for one another, even when things got tough.

In the end, the process of redefining family became a powerful testament to their resilience. They had learned to adapt, to grow, and to find strength in the face of change. Through their letters, journal entries, and shared experiences, Asher, Ethan, and Allison discovered that family was not about being perfect—it was about being present. It was about finding joy in the small moments, creating new traditions, and opening their hearts to the people who had become part of their story.

Their journey, once filled with uncertainty, had brought them to a place of hope. They had redefined what family meant to them, and in doing so, they had discovered a new kind of love—one that was flexible, enduring, and unbreakable.

CHAPTER 8
PART VII: NEW HORIZONS
Embracing a Bicultural Identity

In the quiet moments of reflection, Asher often found himself pondering the complexities of their new life, one that was now shaped by two distinct cultures. His children, Ethan and Allison, were also navigating this new reality, caught between the familiar comfort of their American upbringing and the vibrant, often overwhelming culture of the Philippines. They had left behind the life they had always known, only to discover that their journey wasn't just about adapting to a new country. It was about embracing a bicultural identity—one that honored their past while making room for a future defined by both worlds.

Asher knew that this wouldn't be easy. In the early days, he would sit by the window in their small apartment, writing letters to Ethan and Allison, reminding them of the importance of holding onto their roots. He would describe the familiar smells of the Thanksgiving turkey roasting in the oven, the crackle of fireworks on the Fourth of July, and the comfort of simple things like grilled cheese sandwiches on rainy afternoons. These were the moments that had defined their American life, and he didn't want them to forget.

"Dear Ethan and Allison,

I've been thinking a lot about where we come from and where we are now. It's strange, isn't it? Being in a place that feels so different from everything we've ever known. But I don't want us to lose sight of who we are. We may be far from home, but that doesn't mean we can't carry pieces of it with us. I'll teach you how to make Mama's apple pie this weekend, and we'll tell stories about our time back in California. But I also want you both to know something important—being here, in the Philippines, is a chance for us to grow in ways we never imagined. We can learn from this new culture, make new traditions, and expand who we are."

Asher's words were meant to reassure his children, but even he wasn't immune to the internal struggle that came with balancing two worlds. The desire to hold onto their American identity while immersing themselves in the rich cultural tapestry of the Philippines was a delicate dance. For Ethan, this tension was particularly pronounced. As a teenager, he found himself feeling like an outsider in both places—too American for his new Filipino friends, but increasingly disconnected from the life they had left behind in California.

Ethan's emails to his father captured this struggle with stark honesty.

"Papa,

It's hard. I feel like I don't fit in anywhere. The kids at school are nice, but sometimes they don't get me. I try to explain things, like what Halloween's really like back home, or why we celebrate Thanksgiving, but it feels weird. They laugh, but not in a mean way—just like they don't understand. And sometimes, I don't even understand why I feel so different. I miss things from home, like playing football with my friends and going to In-N-Out after school. It's not like I don't like it here—I do. But there are days when I just want things to be the way they were."

Ethan's words resonated deeply with Asher, who had experienced similar feelings during his own childhood. He remembered growing up with Filipino parents in California, feeling the pull of two cultures and never quite knowing where he belonged. Now, decades later, he watched his son wrestle with the same questions of identity. But there was one key difference—this time, Asher was determined to help Ethan embrace both sides of himself, to see his bicultural identity not as a burden, but as a strength.

"Ethan,

I get it. I know what it's like to feel caught between two places, two cultures. But I want you to know that you don't have to choose one over the other. You can be both. You are both. And that's something to be proud of. Think about it—you have the unique ability to understand two different worlds. You can connect with people in ways that others can't. You're learning things that are going to make you stronger, more adaptable, and more compassionate. I know it doesn't feel like it now, but trust me—you're building something amazing out of these experiences."

Ethan's struggle wasn't isolated. Allison, though younger and more adaptable, had her own moments of confusion. She missed the familiar rhythms of life in California—the smell of pancakes on Saturday mornings, the sound of the school bell signaling recess, and the sight of her old friends on the playground. Yet, Allison was also fascinated by the new world around her. She marveled at the colorful jeepneys that crisscrossed the streets, the exotic fruits at the market, and the rhythmic cadence of Tagalog that filled her ears daily.

In her journal, Allison wrote about the small ways she was learning to blend the two cultures together.

"Today we learned how to say new words in Tagalog, and I'm getting better at it! It's fun because I can teach my new friends words in English, and they teach me words in Tagalog. It's like we're swapping pieces of our worlds. But sometimes I miss things from home. Like, why don't we have peanut butter and jelly sandwiches here? I miss them. Maybe we can make them this weekend, Papa. I'll teach my friends how to make them!"

Allison's enthusiasm for blending cultures was a glimpse into the family's gradual transformation. Over time, their letters and journal entries began to reflect a beautiful merging of their two worlds. The tension that had once defined their bicultural identity started to soften, replaced by a sense of pride and excitement for the new life they were building.

Asher, who had once worried about how his children would adapt, now saw the richness of their experience. He watched as Ethan found his place among his new friends, laughing and joking in a mix of English and Tagalog. He marveled at Allison's ability to straddle both cultures with such ease, blending American customs with the vibrant traditions of the Philippines. And through it all, Asher began to understand that their bicultural identity wasn't something to be resolved—it was something to be embraced.

One evening, after a long day at work, Asher sat down to write another letter to his children. This one, however, felt different. It wasn't about reassuring them or guiding them through the complexities of their dual heritage. This letter was about celebrating who they had become.

"Dear Ethan and Allison,

I want you both to know how proud I am of you. We've been through a lot this past year—so many changes, so many challenges—but look at how far we've come. You've both taken pieces of our old life and woven them into this new one in ways I never could have imagined. Ethan, you've embraced the culture here, learning to speak the language and make new friends, but you've also held onto the things that make you who you are. And Allison, your curiosity and creativity have brought so much light into our lives. You've found ways to blend the best of both worlds, and it's been amazing to watch.

What I've realized is that our blended cultural identity isn't something we have to figure out or balance. It's who we are. It's what makes us special. We're creating a new kind of family—one that's rooted in both American and Filipino traditions, but also entirely our own. And that's something to celebrate."

As Asher wrote, he felt a sense of peace wash over him. They had come a long way from those early days of confusion and uncertainty. They were no longer clinging to the past or struggling to fit into their new surroundings. Instead, they were creating something new—something that honored both their American roots and their Filipino present. It was a journey that had taken time, patience, and a lot of love, but they had made it.

Ethan's response to his father's letter was short, but it spoke volumes.

"Papa,

I'm starting to get it now. We don't have to pick one or the other. We can be both. I've been thinking about how cool it is that I know stuff my friends here don't, and they know stuff I don't. We're learning from each other. And that's pretty awesome. Thanks for helping me see that."

For Allison, the blending of cultures was something she had always embraced, even if she hadn't realized it at first. Her journal entries became filled with colorful descriptions of her favorite Filipino dishes—lumpia, adobo, and halo-halo—alongside her cravings for American classics like mac and cheese and chocolate chip cookies. She was learning to love both sides of herself, understanding that she didn't have to choose between them.

As the months passed, the family continued to grow into their bicultural identity, finding joy in the small moments that bridged their two worlds. They celebrated both American and Filipino holidays, sharing Thanksgiving dinners with new friends while embracing local festivals like Sinulog and Pahiyas. Their home was a blend of both cultures—a place where American recipes were cooked alongside Filipino dishes, where English and Tagalog intertwined effortlessly.

Their journey of healing and adaptation had led them to a place of acceptance—acceptance of their past, their present, and the unique future they were building together. They no longer saw their bicultural identity as a source of conflict. Instead, it had become a wellspring of strength, offering them the chance to connect with people from all walks of life and to see the world through a richer, more nuanced lens.

The family realized that embracing their dual cultural identity wasn't about choosing one culture over the other. It was about blending the best of both worlds to create something unique, something entirely their own. Through this journey, they found not just a stronger sense of belonging, but a future bursting with endless possibilities. They stood tall, proud of who they had become, and together, with renewed strength, they declared, "We are Filipino Americans!"

DREAMS FOR THE FUTURE

As the evening sun cast long shadows across the room, Asher sat at his small desk, staring at a blank page in front of him. The weight of everything he had been through—the divorce, the move to the Philippines, the months of struggling to find work—pressed heavily on his shoulders. But this letter, this moment, wasn't about the past. It was about the future. His future, Ethan's future, and Allison's future. After everything they had endured, Asher wanted to give his children something powerful: hope.

He had spent so many nights wrestling with his demons, the depression that had taken hold of him after the divorce, threatening to pull him under. The quiet despair of failing to find a job when they first arrived in the Philippines had left him feeling helpless. Asher had always prided himself on being the provider, the one who could keep things together, but in those early months, it felt like everything was falling apart. Every rejection, every "We'll get back to you," hit him like a hammer, each blow driving him further into doubt.

But there was something that kept him going—something that always brought him back from the edge. His kids. Ethan and Allison were the reason he got out of bed every morning, the reason he pushed through the fog of depression, the reason he refused to give up. They had been through so much, and they were watching him. He couldn't let them down.

And so, Asher began to write, pouring his dreams for their future onto the page, determined to give them a vision of hope and possibility, even if his own path had been filled with struggle.

"Dear Ethan and Allison,

There's something I want you both to know. No matter what we've been through, no matter how hard things have gotten, I believe in you. I believe in the strength you have, the resilience you've shown, and the incredible future that's waiting for you. You are capable of so much, and I want you to dream big. I want you to see the world not just for what it is, but for what it could be, because you have the power to shape it."

As Asher wrote, he thought back to the days when he had struggled to find his footing after they moved. He had sat in countless interviews, wearing the same suit he had brought from California, feeling the same knot of anxiety in his stomach. It wasn't just about finding a job; it was about proving to himself that he could still provide for his family, still be the father they needed him to be.

There were times he wanted to give up, to throw in the towel and admit defeat. But every time he looked at Ethan and Allison, he knew he had to keep fighting. They were counting on him, and he couldn't let them see him fall. It had taken months, but eventually, he found work. It wasn't glamorous, and it wasn't what he had envisioned when they first moved, but it was enough to keep them afloat. And from that point, things had slowly begun to improve.

Now, as he sat there writing to his children, Asher knew that the most important lesson he could give them was the one he had learned himself: no matter how dark things got, there was always light on the other side. They had survived, and now it was time to dream again.

"I want you to know that your dreams matter," he continued, his handwriting steady now. "Whether you want to become a doctor, an artist, a teacher, or something else entirely, I will be there to support you every step of the way. Don't let the challenges we've faced hold you back. Use them to push you forward. You've seen how tough life can be, but you've also seen how strong we are. You've seen how, even when things seem impossible, we find a way."

Asher paused, thinking about Ethan. His son had been through so much. The divorce had hit him hard, and the move had only added to the confusion and anger he felt. But over the past few months, Asher had seen Ethan begin to change. He was growing into a young man who was not only thoughtful but also deeply empathetic, shaped by the challenges they had faced as a family.

Ethan's response to Asher's letter arrived a few days later, a reflection of his own hopes and dreams, but also of the wisdom he had gained from their shared struggles.

"Papa,

I've been thinking a lot about what you said. It's hard to imagine the future sometimes because the past feels so heavy, but you're right. We've been through a lot, and we're still standing. I don't know exactly what I want to do yet, but I know that I want to make a difference. I want to help people the way you've helped me. I think about how hard it was when we first got here, how you kept going even when things were tough, and I want to be like that. I want to make sure that whatever I do, I'm giving back, helping others find their way, just like we've been finding ours."

Ethan's words filled Asher with a deep sense of pride. His son had taken their struggles and turned them into something powerful—an ambition to make the world a better place. It was more than Asher could have hoped for, and it reminded him that the tough times they had faced had shaped Ethan into someone compassionate and strong. Asher's dreams for Ethan had always been simple: he wanted his son to be happy, to find his place in the world. Now, it seemed that Ethan was starting to carve that path for himself.

Allison's dreams, too, were beginning to take shape. At seven, she was still young, but her journal entries revealed a growing understanding of the world around her. She wrote about her love of painting, of how she wanted to create art that would bring people together, just like she had brought her own family together with her colorful portraits.

In one of her entries, she described a painting she had been working on—a depiction of their life in California alongside their new life in the Philippines, both places intertwined in a swirl of colors.

"Papa,

I painted something today that I want to show you! It's of our old house and our new one, but they're together, like they're part of the same picture. I think it's like us—we have two places we belong to now, and that makes us special. I want to keep painting pictures like this, ones that show how different places and people can come together. And maybe one day, I'll help other families who have to move like we did. I'll show them how to bring their homes with them, no matter where they go."

Asher smiled as he read her words. Allison's dreams were filled with the kind of hope and creativity that only a child could possess, but they also carried a deeper message. She was beginning to understand the importance of bridging cultures, of finding beauty in the connections between worlds. Her paintings weren't just about art—they were about healing, about showing people that no matter where life took them, they could always carry their past with them while embracing their future.

As the months went by, Asher's letters to Ethan and Allison became less about guidance and more about celebration. They had come so far as a family, and he wanted them to know how proud he was—not just of their resilience, but of their dreams, their ambitions, and the incredible people they were becoming.

In one of his final letters, Asher summed up the dreams he had for their future.

"Dear Ethan and Allison,

I hope you both know how proud I am of you. I've watched you grow, not just as my children, but as individuals with your own unique dreams and strengths. Ethan, your desire to help others is something that will carry you far in life. And Allison, your creativity and kindness will touch more people than you know. My dream for both of you is that you continue to follow your passions, no matter where they take you. And remember this: no matter what happens, no matter where life leads us, we will always be a family. That is something no challenge can ever take away from us."

Asher's words echoed a truth he had come to understand during the darkest moments of his depression: dreams are what keep you moving forward. They are what give you hope when everything feels impossible. And now, as he looked toward the future, he knew that their family's journey—filled with adversity, heartache, and growth—had only made them stronger.

Ethan and Allison's responses, filled with excitement and possibility, reflected the powerful impact of Asher's belief in them. Ethan wrote about his plans to volunteer at local organizations, inspired by his father's resilience. Allison's journal entries continued to brim with new ideas for paintings, each one capturing the essence of the life they were building together.

Together, they were a family reborn, defined not by the hardships they had faced, but by the dreams they had for the future. Asher had always believed in his children's potential, but now, seeing the strength they had gained through their shared experiences, he knew that the future was brighter than ever.

In the end, it wasn't just about the dreams they had as individuals—it was about the dreams they shared as a family. A future filled with love, success, and personal fulfillment. A future where they could look back at the obstacles they had overcome and know, without a doubt, that they had made it through together.

And as Asher folded his final letter, sealing it with a sense of peace, he whispered the words that had carried them this far: "We will always be a family."

CHAPTER 9
EPILOGUE: LETTERS OF HOPE

Asher's Letter to His Future Self

Dear Future Asher,

As I sit here, reflecting on the chaos and uncertainty that life has thrown our way, the weight of everything that's happened presses heavily on me. The divorce, the move, the struggles to rebuild—it all feels overwhelming at times. But even with this heavy heart, an inexplicable hope rises within me. I'm writing this letter not just to remind myself of where we've been, but to speak to you—the person I hope I will become—so that you remember the strength it took to get here and the dreams that carried us forward.

The divorce has left its mark on Ethan, Allison, and me, but I refuse to let it define who we are. It won't be the end of our story. This move to the Philippines, though terrifying at first, has been more than just a change of scenery. It's a chance to start over, to build something stronger than what we had before. I hope that when you read this, you'll remember just how far we've come.

Have we found the strength to overcome what once seemed insurmountable? Have we created a home where Ethan and Allison feel safe, where they can dream and grow without the weight of the past holding them down? I hope that by the time you read this, their laughter fills our home again, and the pain in their eyes has softened, replaced by the sparkle of new adventures and possibilities.

You've been through hell, Asher, and the weight of single parenthood can be consuming. But remember, you've never been alone. Ethan and Allison have been watching you, drawing strength from your determination. They've seen you struggle to find work, to piece together a life for them amidst uncertainty. And through it all, they've seen you show up for them, day after day. That's what matters—not the mistakes, not the doubts, but the fact that you never stopped trying.

I'm writing to remind you: You're doing enough. Even when it feels like the weight of the world is on your shoulders, you are doing enough. Single parenthood is hard, but it's also filled with moments of grace. The small victories—Ethan opening up to you, Allison surprising you with her drawings—are reminders that you're building something beautiful, even in the midst of hardship.

There have been nights when you lay awake, wondering if you're making the right decisions. Wondering if you'll ever give your children the life they deserve. But Asher—you already have. It's not about the material things, the perfect house, or the job that pays the bills. It's about the love you've given them, the way you've shown up, the way you've allowed them to see you be both vulnerable and strong.

By now, I hope you've learned to forgive yourself for the things you couldn't control. The divorce, the move, the uncertainty of starting over—none of it was easy. But you survived. More than that, you've taught Ethan and Allison how to survive too. You've shown them what it means to be resilient, to keep going even when the road ahead seems uncertain. And in doing so, you've given them the greatest gift—the belief that they can face anything life throws their way.

But this journey isn't just about surviving. It's about thriving. It's about finding joy in the small moments, in the laughter that now fills your home, in the friendships you've built in this new land. I hope you've found a balance between holding on to your roots and embracing the rich Filipino culture that now surrounds you.

You've learned something important along this journey: Family isn't defined by circumstance. It's defined by love, by how you've held each other up when everything else seemed to fall apart. You've built a new kind of family, one rooted in strength and resilience. And isn't that the greatest lesson? Even in the face of overwhelming odds, you've not only survived—you've found a way to thrive.

This letter is for those moments when you feel like you're sinking, questioning whether you're doing enough. For the nights when doubt creeps in, wondering if the kids are okay, if you're providing all they need. It's a reminder that, in those quiet hours, you're not alone. What you're doing is enough.

Single parenthood isn't easy, but it's filled with moments of incredible strength. There will be times when the weight feels unbearable, when exhaustion takes over and you don't know how you'll keep going. But you will. You'll find strength in the smallest things—in a quiet moment with your children, in the way they look at you with love and trust, in the way you've built a life for them, even when you thought you couldn't.

By the time you read this, I hope you look back with pride. I hope you see how far we've come, how much we've grown, and how the pain that once felt insurmountable has transformed into something beautiful. I hope you've found peace, knowing that, despite everything, we've created a life filled with love, laughter, and possibility.

Starting over is terrifying, but it's also filled with hope. The hope that comes from knowing the future is unwritten and that we have the power to shape it with every choice we make. I know we're going to create something amazing out of this life, because we already have.

In those moments of struggle, pain, and exhaustion, remember that you're not alone. Your challenges are real, and so is your strength. Your love is what will carry you through, even when everything feels like it's falling apart. You are enough—more than enough—and even in the hardest times, you are building something beautiful.

This journey is hard, but it's filled with moments of grace. Hold on to those moments, the ones that remind you why you keep going. The ones that show, no matter how difficult the road, you are moving forward. And in that steady, unyielding progress, there is hope. There is always hope.

With love and strength,
Asher - 2016

As Asher folded the letter, he felt the weight lift from his chest. The future was uncertain, yes, but it was also filled with possibility. He didn't know what lay ahead, but he knew one thing for sure: they would face it together. Ethan, Allison, and him. A family, stronger than ever before, ready to take on the world.

And as he placed the letter in the drawer, a quiet smile crossed his face. He had faced the worst of it and come out on the other side. They had all come out stronger. And no matter what challenges lay ahead, Asher knew they would not just survive—they would thrive.

ETHAN AND ALLISON'S JOINT MESSAGE

In the quiet of their new home, Ethan and Allison sat together, writing a letter that would become a turning point in their family's story. It wasn't just any letter—it was a joint message to their Papa, Asher. What had started as a simple idea between the siblings quickly grew into something deeper, something that captured the essence of their journey. Together, they reflected on the rollercoaster ride they'd been on since moving to the Philippines, and as their thoughts spilled onto the page, it became clear that this letter would be a celebration of everything they had become—a family reshaped by challenges but strengthened by love.

Ethan began the letter, his words carrying the weight of his newfound maturity. He had always been the protective big brother, but the move and the divorce had forced him to grow up faster than he'd imagined. As he wrote, he found himself reflecting on how much his father's strength had meant to him during those tough times.

Dear Papa,

It feels strange writing this with Allison, but in a good way. We've been talking a lot lately about everything that's happened, and I wanted to start by saying something I haven't said enough: thank you. I used to think that being strong meant keeping everything inside, but I've realized that strength is also about letting people in. You taught me that without even knowing it.

I know I wasn't always easy to deal with after we left LA. There were times when I was angry, confused, and didn't understand why things had to change so much. But looking back now, I see how hard you worked to hold everything together. I see the late nights, the job struggles, and the way you always made sure we had what we needed, even when I was too wrapped up in my own world to notice. I know now that you were carrying a lot more than we realized.

As Ethan paused, Allison leaned over and added her part. At just seven years old, she had a way of seeing the world through a lens of hope and joy. She was the one who often brought lightness to their home, even in the darkest moments. Her words were simpler, but they carried a sincerity that tugged at the heart.

Papa,

I love you so much. You always tell me that I'm brave, but I think you're the bravest of all! You brought us all the way here to the Philippines, and I know it wasn't easy for you, but you did it because you love us. I miss Mama sometimes, and I know you do too, but you make sure we're happy and safe. I like it here now, and I know you worked really hard to make this place feel like home.

Do you remember when we first got here, and I was scared because everything was so different? You told me that change can be good, even if it's hard at first. You were right, Papa. I've made friends, I've learned new things, and I even like some of the food now! I still miss peanut butter sandwiches though, but it's okay because you always find a way to make things fun.

Ethan smiled as he read Allison's words, feeling a swell of pride for his little sister. She had been through so much, and yet here she was, bouncing back with her usual optimism. Ethan continued writing, this time with a lighter tone, reflecting on how the two of them had become each other's greatest allies during this transition.

Papa,

Allison's right—you are the bravest of us all. And while it wasn't always easy, I think we're better for it. Moving here wasn't just about starting over in a new place. It was about us becoming a stronger family. Allison and I have gotten closer in ways I never expected. We've had to rely on each other more, whether it's helping with school, figuring out new customs, or just talking about what we miss from home.

It wasn't just about getting used to a new country—it was about figuring out how to move forward together, as a family. You showed us what it means to keep going, even when it feels like everything's up in the air. And I want you to know, we see it. We see all the things you've done for us, the sacrifices you made to get us to where we are today.

Allison piped up again, her handwriting a bit larger than her brother's, but no less important.

Papa,

Ethan says I've been brave, but he's been my hero. He helps me when I feel scared or when I don't understand something at school. We've had some hard days, but he always finds a way to make me laugh. We've talked a lot about what we want to do when we grow up. I want to help other kids who move to new places like we did, so they don't feel scared like I did at first.

Ethan nodded at his sister's words, feeling the same surge of pride he had felt earlier. He took over the letter again, this time writing about their shared dreams for the future.

Papa,

We've been talking a lot about what's next, and I think we both have some big dreams. Allison's already told you hers, but I want you to know that I've been thinking about how I can give back too. I want to do something that makes a difference—whether it's through helping others or maybe even doing something to bridge the cultures we're part of. Moving here has shown me how important it is to be open to new things and new people. You've shown us that. I want to take what we've learned and use it to make the world a little better.

As Ethan's words flowed onto the page, he realized just how much they had all grown. This move had been difficult, but it had also brought them closer. It had given them a new understanding of who they were as a family, and what they were capable of overcoming together.

In the final part of their letter, Ethan and Allison wrote together, their thoughts aligned as they reflected on what the future might hold.

Papa,

We want you to know that no matter what happens next, we're ready for it. You've taught us that challenges aren't something to fear—they're something to learn from. We've seen you go through tough times and still find a way to smile and make sure we're okay. We're stronger because of it.

We want to make you proud, not just by doing well in school or following our dreams, but by being kind and brave, just like you. We're going to keep our traditions alive—both the ones from home and the ones we're learning here in the Philippines. We'll never forget where we came from, but we're excited about where we're going.

Thank you for everything, Papa. For loving us, for believing in us, and for showing us that no matter how hard things get, family is what matters most. We love you.

As they finished the letter, Ethan and Allison sat back, feeling a deep sense of satisfaction. This wasn't just a message to their father—it was a celebration of how far they had come as a family. The move, the divorce, the challenges of a new culture—none of it had broken them. In fact, it had only brought them closer.

Together, they had learned to navigate the complexities of life with grace and resilience. And through their words, they hoped to remind their father that his sacrifices hadn't gone unnoticed. They had become stronger, not just because of him, but because of the love and support they had for each other.

The joint message was more than a letter—it was a symbol of unity, of a family that had been through the fire and come out stronger on the other side. And as they sealed the envelope and placed it on their father's desk, Ethan and Allison shared a look that spoke volumes: they were ready for whatever came next.

Their journey wasn't over, but they knew one thing for sure: they would face the future together, with love, courage, and hope. And that was more than enough.

A FAMILY UNITED

A year had passed since Asher, Ethan, and Allison had made the monumental move to the Philippines, and the air in their new home carried a different weight now—one not of uncertainty and fear, but of contentment and hope. The once daunting transition had evolved into a journey that reshaped them into something stronger, something unbreakable. As they stood at the precipice of a new chapter, they knew they had crossed an invisible threshold, their hearts and lives forever intertwined by the challenges they had faced together.

Their letters, which once felt like lifelines connecting distant hearts across the emotional miles, now sat in a small, worn box on the corner of Asher's desk. They were no longer needed in the same way. Instead of serving as bridges across divides, the letters had become symbols of their shared growth, resilience, and the strength of their family. They were a record of the moments that had forged them into the family they were today—one that wasn't defined by circumstance but by the unbreakable bond of love.

Asher leaned back in his chair, eyes closed for a moment, letting the sounds of the home he had rebuilt wash over him. The clatter of dishes as Ethan helped Allison set the table for dinner, the soft hum of music in the background, and the occasional burst of laughter—it was the sound of peace. The sound of family. It hadn't been easy getting here, but it was moments like this that reminded him it had all been worth it.

Ethan had grown in ways Asher could never have imagined. He wasn't the confused, angry boy he had been when they first arrived. No longer lost between two worlds, Ethan had found his place, his confidence shining through everything he did. He excelled at school, not just academically but socially, making friends and immersing himself in the new culture. Ethan had become a leader, someone his classmates looked up to. He had found his voice in this new world and, more importantly, had learned to appreciate the duality of his identity as both American and Filipino.

As Asher watched him now, joking with Allison as they folded napkins together, he marveled at how far his son had come. Ethan had discovered a strength within himself that even Asher hadn't fully seen before. He had found his way through the confusion and the pain, and come out the other side with a quiet determination to build a life on his terms.

"Papa, dinner's ready!" Allison's voice interrupted his thoughts, and Asher smiled.

Allison, the little girl who once clung to him in fear of the unknown, had blossomed into a joyful, curious, and resilient young girl. The move hadn't been easy for her either, but where Ethan had struggled with anger, Allison had quietly processed the changes, finding solace in her art. Her paintings now filled the walls of their home, vibrant depictions of both their life in California and their new experiences in the Philippines. Each brushstroke told a story—of longing, of healing, of joy. And as Asher gazed at the newest one, a family portrait where the lines of their old and new worlds blended together seamlessly, he felt an overwhelming sense of pride.

As they gathered around the dinner table, the simple act of sitting down together felt like the culmination of a journey. It was a moment of unity, a symbol of how far they had come as a family. The food was a blend of the old and the new—a mix of American dishes alongside Filipino favorites that they had learned to love. Ethan and Allison chatted animatedly about their day, their excitement spilling over in waves of laughter. They were happy. Truly happy.

Asher's heart swelled as he watched them. They had faced so much together—the pain of divorce, the fear of starting over in a foreign land, the struggles of adapting to a new culture. But instead of breaking them, those challenges had forged something stronger. They had become a unit, each supporting the other through the ups and downs, each growing in ways that Asher could never have predicted. They weren't just surviving anymore—they were thriving.

"Papa," Ethan began, his voice steady and confident. "I was thinking about the move, and, you know, I used to hate it. I thought it was the worst thing that could happen to us. But now… I see why we had to do it. It's made us stronger, hasn't it?"

Asher nodded, his throat tight with emotion. "It has, Ethan. It really has."

"I get it now," Ethan continued. "Change is hard, but it doesn't have to be bad. It's what we make of it, right?"

"Exactly," Asher said, his voice thick with pride. "It's about what we make of it."

Allison chimed in, her face lighting up. "And look how much fun we've had! We've learned so many new things. I love my school, and I love painting with the kids next door. We're a part of something bigger now."

Asher smiled at his daughter's enthusiasm. "Yes, we are. We've found a new kind of family here."

And in that moment, it became clear—family wasn't just the three of them sitting around the table. It was the neighbors who had welcomed them with open arms, the teachers who had gone out of their way to help Ethan and Allison adjust, the community that had embraced them as one of their own. Their family had expanded in ways Asher hadn't expected. They had found their place in this new world, and it had become home.

But as the conversation ebbed and flowed, and as the dinner drew to a close, Asher knew that this wasn't the end of their story. It was just the beginning of a new chapter. The challenges they had faced had shaped them, yes, but they hadn't defined them. They had become stronger because of the struggles, and now, with their hearts and minds open to the future, anything was possible.

After dinner, as Ethan and Allison cleared the table, Asher sat back for a moment, letting the warmth of the evening settle over him. He thought back to the letter he had written to his future self just over a year ago. The Asher who had written that letter was full of fear and uncertainty, unsure of how they would make it through. But the Asher sitting here now—he was different. He was proud. He was hopeful.

He stood up and walked over to the desk where the old box of letters sat. Carefully, he opened it, rifling through the memories of the past year—the words that had carried them through the hardest times. Asher pulled out the letter he had written to himself and smiled as he unfolded it. He didn't need to read it. He knew what it said. It had been a letter of hope, a promise to himself that they would get through it. And now, standing in the light of their new life, he knew he had kept that promise.

He folded the letter back up and placed it in the box, closing it gently. There would be more letters, more stories to tell, but this chapter of their lives had come to a close. They had faced their fears, they had found their strength, and they had come out the other side as a family united.

Ethan and Allison joined him in the living room, and Asher pulled them close, wrapping his arms around both of them. The weight of the past year—the struggles, the heartache, the uncertainty—seemed to dissolve in that moment. All that remained was love. Pure, unwavering love.

"I love you both," Asher said softly, his voice thick with emotion.

"We love you too, Papa," they replied in unison, their voices filled with the warmth of home.

They sat there, together, for a long time, basking in the quiet joy of the moment. The future stretched out before them, filled with possibility and hope. They didn't know what it would bring, but they knew one thing for sure: whatever came next, they would face it together.

And as the night settled around them, Asher realized something important—it wasn't about where they had been or even where they were going. It was about who they had become along the way. A family, united by love, shaped by resilience, and bound by the unbreakable threads of their shared journey.

Their story wasn't over. In fact, it was just beginning.

And in that beginning, Asher, Ethan, and Allison knew they could face anything.

Together.

Allan Q. Amit

Allan Q. Amit is a highly accomplished C-level executive with a wealth of experience in leadership and community engagement. He has a proven track record of success in leading organizations, including his role as the Charter President of the L.A. Synergy Lions Club, the 2nd Vice President of the Filipino American Chamber of Commerce, and a Board Director of Friends of Echo Park Library. With his exceptional ability to build effective teams and collaborate with other organizations, Allan has consistently delivered results that exceed expectations.

In addition, Allan's expertise in business and entrepreneurship is widely recognized. He has been invited to share his valuable insights and guidance to startups and small businesses as a guest speaker on the podcast "What to Look for When Hiring a Virtual Assistant for Your Small Business." Allan's commitment to promoting literacy and cultural representation in children's literature is also noteworthy. His media appearances, live readings, and collaborations with The Yellow Boat Project and Green Mango Books have made a positive impact in the community.

As a C-level executive, Allan's exceptional leadership, communication, and community engagement skills are unparalleled. His experience and expertise will undoubtedly help drive success and growth in any company or organization he is a part of.

AWARDS & RECOGNITION

- U.S. House of Representatives
- California Legislature Assembly Recognition – 2015 & 2016
- City of Los Angeles Recognition – 2015
- City of Cerritos, California Recognition – 2014

- Special Recognition – Lions Club International 2015 & 2016
- United Chamber of Commerce of San Fernando Valley.
- Small Business Award winner - 2015

CAREER

As a seasoned C-level executive, Allan Q. Amit brings over 15 years of experience in leadership, change management, project management, cost control, and process improvement. His strategic thinking and results-driven approach have enabled him to drive revenue growth, improve productivity, and enhance service quality in previous roles. Throughout his career, Allan has held various leadership positions, including MIS Department Head at C2H Inc., Managing Consultant, Co-Founder and General Manager of Green Mango Books, and Team Manager at Bank of America. In these roles, he has spearheaded the creation of new departments, developed long-term strategies, streamlined processes, implemented technology solutions, and managed teams to achieve operational excellence.

Allan is a natural leader with strong communication skills and cross-cultural competencies. His talent for conflict resolution and promoting collaboration and constructive dialogue have made him an asset in any team environment. He has mentored and coached team members to improve their skills and fostered a culture of continuous learning and development..

CONSULTANT SINCE 2005

As a consultant, Allan has helped clients collect business information, analyze and interpret data to identify problems and formulate solutions in concise reports. He has guided and resolved any issues that may arise while selecting and coaching clients' managers and supervisors. He has also developed innovative systems and reporting tools to create a data-rich environment for clients. Allan's expertise in leadership, project management, and process improvement has helped clients achieve their goals and drive growth.

Allan's diverse background and experience in developing and executing long-term strategies, streamlining processes, and implementing technology solutions make him a valuable asset to any organization. Being a consultant since 2005 to BPO companies, he can provide strategic guidance in improving any business processes and optimizing operations. With his excellent communication skills and cross-cultural competencies, Allan can effectively collaborate with any team and foster a culture of continuous improvement.

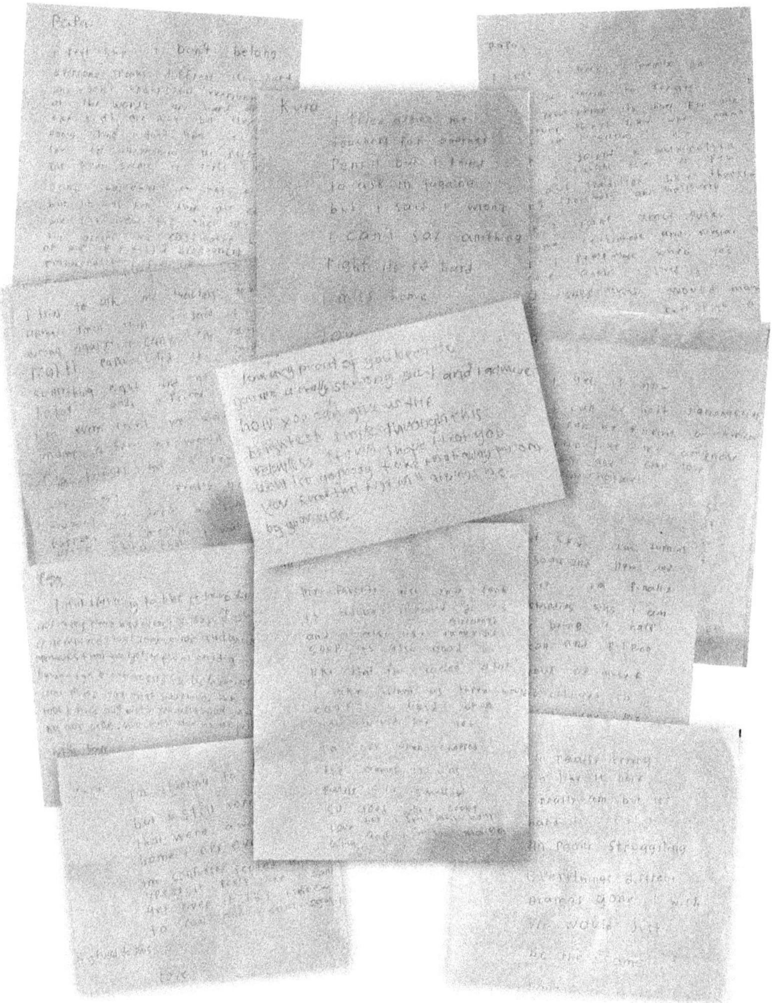
I can't say anything
and I admire
by your side.